GHOST!

Poltergeist

Titles in the Ghosthunters series

GHOSTHUNTERS

Poltergeist

Anthony Masters

 ORCHARD BOOKS

ORCHARD BOOKS
96 Leonard Street, London EC2A 4RH
Orchard Books Australia
14 Mars Road, Lane Cove, NSW 2066
ISBN 1 86039 814 6
First published in Great Britain in 1996
First paperback publication 1996
This paperback edition 1998
Text © Anthony Masters 1996
A CIP catalogue record for this book is available from the
British Library.
Printed in Great Britain

To the staff and pupils of Eastbrook
Comprehensive School, Dagenham, Essex,
with affectionate memories of their outstanding
creative work

CHAPTER ONE

The noise was incredible and so was Mr Golding's shout of alarm. When David and Jenny clambered up into the attic they saw an amazing sight. Balls were bouncing, a model train was whizzing round the track, a clockwork caterpillar arched its way through their father's legs and with sudden ferocity a bat hit a cricket ball straight through the window with a crash of broken glass.

Then, just as suddenly, the room was still except for a burst of delighted laughter that was cut off immediately.

"Well, I'm–" Mr Golding's back was pressed against the wall and he was staring down at the still ball, the silent train, the unmoving caterpillar and the innocent-looking bat. 'What was all that about?" He was terrified.

The twins gazed back at him, unable to understand what had caused the commotion but feeling as shocked and fearful as their father. Had these things really moved? It didn't seem possible.

"I don't believe it," Mr Golding was saying. "I just don't get it."

"I saw them too, Dad," said David. "At least I think I did."

"Look at the window," said Jenny impatiently. "It's broken."

It was.

David was convinced now. But had his father heard the laughter? He was sure Jenny had. "Did you hear anything else, anything strange?"

"What do you mean?" asked his father suspiciously.

"Like laughter?" he said reluctantly.

"No. I didn't hear any laughter." He was amazed and then angry. "Wait a minute – has all this funny business got something to do with you two? If so, I don't call it a joke. Not with me slaving my fingers to the bone trying to get this old place to rights. Maybe you'd like to be back on the estate. Maybe–"

"Dad!" Jenny protested. "We didn't do anything."

Mr Golding gazed down at the clockwork caterpillar as if it was going to attack him at any moment. "You didn't?"

"You know we didn't," said David. "How could we?"

"Mmm. Must have been the electrics."

"The electrics?"

"Yeah. Whole place needs rewiring."

"How could–" David began, but Jenny nudged her brother hard. If their father needed a rational explanation, however far-fetched, then he had to have it. For his own sake. How could *he* believe in the supernatural? Only they had experience of it.[1] Yet he had seen it all but hadn't heard the laughter. She wondered what that meant.

"There must be an explanation," Mr Golding continued, gradually talking himself back into confidence. "I know – what about static electricity?"

"But how can–" began David. This time Jenny kicked him.

"Aren't we going to clear up all this stuff?" she asked.

Her father shook his head. "Don't seem right to touch it. Not yet anyway. I'm still trying to contact the Frasers – they were the last owners."

After a long period out of work when his building business went bankrupt, Mr Golding had landed a job as manager of a garden centre that bordered the Thames. He had always loved gardening and the family was certain he would make a success of it, but Reg Golding had lost so much confidence by being unemployed that he wasn't so sure. Nevertheless, he had let their small

[1] Haunted School.

3

estate house and they moved into River House, the dilapidated, three-storeyed Victorian building that went with the job.

The place had been empty for years, except for a little attic room that was still mysteriously full of toys. David and Jenny had often wondered why, but however hard they tried to find out, their father had only made vague references to the last owners having left "quickly". Now, from the confiding look in his eyes, they knew that they were going to get an explanation at last.

"Who were the Frasers, Dad?" asked David.

"Don't know much about them." He paused almost guiltily. "They lived here and ran the centre, but when they went it was just left to become derelict. Then Thames Garden Centres bought the lot. All I was told was that we could move in but I'd have to try and fix up the place myself." He paused. "Mr Davis did say the attic was full of a load of junk and we could get rid of it if we liked."

"Junk?" David was suddenly angry. "That's not junk."

"Don't you know any more about these Frasers?" Jenny persisted. "Didn't anyone tell you anything else?"

"No," he repeated firmly.

"So how will you contact them?"

"What's this," he asked grumpily, "the Inquisition?"

"Please, Dad," Jenny implored him.

"I don't have the time, do I?"

"When did the Frasers move out?" asked Jenny.

"Years ago now."

"But there's not much dust up here," she said.

"I gave everything a bit of a clean, didn't I?" replied Mr Golding awkwardly. "Wasn't right – leaving them in a state."

Jenny went over and kissed him on the cheek. Dad was a real sentimentalist. That was why they loved him so much.

David and Jenny went for a walk on the path by the Thames to have a talk and a think about what had happened. Old hulks of barges lay rotting in the mud and deserted wharves led down to the Royal Naval dockyard, which was being turned into a museum. The whole area had been described by the local council as a "dockyard regeneration site", but the only business to be re-established so far had been the garden centre.

"Do you know what I reckon that was?" said David, looking up at the smashed attic window. Then he started to hunt in the long, salty, ragged grass.

"Poltergeist?" she asked.

"Yeah." He looked disappointed, having hoped to surprise her.

"Restless spirit?"

"Could be. Certainly wasn't electricity – static or otherwise. That's just Dad trying to convince himself."

"Why do you think it's started up now?" Jenny wondered. "After all, we've been here for six months."

"When did Dad dust those toys?"

"Recently, I think," said Jenny. "So maybe he woke some spirit."

"Or showed that someone cared."

"Do you think he feels deserted, whoever he is?" Jenny was immediately full of concern.

"He feels something," replied David. "But *what* I don't know," he added ominously. Then he found the cricket ball under some old netting. "Here it is. Not bad, is it?" He tossed it up and down and then dropped the ball with a howl.

"What's the matter?"

"It burnt me."

Jenny knelt down beside the cricket ball and tapped it quickly with one finger. It was still hot, but when she looked at David's hand there wasn't a mark on it.

"Can't have been that bad," she said.

"It hurt." David was furious there was nothing to show for his pain. "That kid's playing tricks."

"Jenny."

"Mmm?"

"Jenny, wake up!"

She turned over sleepily to see her brother standing by the bedside. He looked upset.

"What is it?" She sat up blearily.

"I can hear sobbing."

"Sobbing? Is Mum unhappy?"

"Don't be daft. It's not her – or Dad."

"Then who?"

"It's the poltergeist."

Jenny looked at her brother sharply. "*I* can't hear crying."

"You will if you stand by the attic stairs," he snapped. "Come on! You've got to get up."

As they stood at the bottom of the flight of wooden stairs without hearing anything, Jenny glanced at her watch. It was 3 a.m. David must have been dreaming. She told him so, but he brushed her aside irritably.

"I could hear him."

"Keep quiet – you'll wake Mum and Dad."

"Let's go up, then." David was insistent now. "We can't just leave him up there, being unhappy. Crying."

"OK." She sighed and followed her twin up the stairs. He sometimes sensed more than she did. Not much more but– Then she, too, heard the sobbing. It was soft and painful.

"There!" David was triumphant.

"Open the door, then," she said impatiently, but he paused, hesitating at the last moment, and Jenny pushed past him, opening it gently, her heart thumping.

The boy was lying on the floor, playing with some soldiers. His shape seemed a little hazy, almost there but not quite. He was sobbing quietly, the tears running down his face, and he didn't look up.

The twins hovered uncertainly in the doorway, wondering what to do next. Then the boy picked up a drawing pad and a crayon. On the white paper he scrawled a name: JACK.

"Jack," breathed David. "Can you hear me, Jack? Can you see me?"

But the boy didn't look up and the twins shivered, for suddenly the room seemed to have become deathly cold.

"Can you hear us?" asked Jenny.

But he gave no impression of hearing anyone, and when he had written his name he returned to playing with his soldiers, his body looking more insubstantial than ever. Nevertheless, they could see that he was about their age, short but well-built with a mop of unruly red hair.

"What shall we do?" Jenny asked.

"He can't hear or see us," said David. "But he must be able to sense us, or why would he have written his name?"

Jenny nodded, seeing the logic of what he said but still not knowing what to do. Then David had an idea. Slowly, cautiously, he picked his way over the toys and knelt down beside Jack.

He picked up the drawing pad and the crayon and wrote down his own name and Jenny's. Then he pushed the pad towards the boy, taking care not to knock over his soldiers.

The boy didn't look at the pad immediately, and even when he did he merely glanced at it casually and then continued with his game.

"He can't see," whispered Jenny.

"Wait!"

Slowly Jack was picking up the crayon again. He wrote, PLAY WITH ME.

They both hesitated, then turned as they heard a sound behind them. The model engine had started up and was pulling its coaches round the track. When David and Jenny looked back, Jack had gone. Only the drawing pad remained with the three names on it.

★

"How can we play with him?" asked Jenny as they cautiously returned to David's room. They both felt stunned and somehow sad, as if an old friend had disappeared.

"I'll give him a game," said David.

"What of?"

"Well, I could give him a game of cricket."

"In the attic?"

"French cricket, then. He's obviously got a good eye for a ball. Or do you think he'll try and burn me again?"

"Not if he trusts you," said Jenny hopefully. "When are you going to give him his game?"

"Tomorrow perhaps."

"Don't forget Auntie Joan's coming."

"Oh, no!" David was instantly depressed.

Auntie Joan was their father's older sister – a widow who was inclined to be both fussy and bossy and who also took offence very easily.

"That won't make any difference." David made a decision. "I'll go up late at night. Like now."

"Can I come?" Jenny realised she was no longer afraid but jealous.

"Of course," replied David.

Did he really want her, she wondered.

Auntie Joan seemed more irritating than ever when she arrived in the middle of the afternoon.

She was small, with darting, questioning eyes, and always wanted to know everyone's private business.

While their mother showed her round, the twins sat in the kitchen, praying she would not be rash enough to take her sister-in-law up to the attic. If she did, there was no doubt that Auntie Joan would start interfering. She'd never let the subject rest; Auntie Joan invariably followed everything through to the bitter end.

"Are you afraid of Jack?" asked Jenny curiously.

"A bit," replied David reluctantly. "But we've got to get through to him. He seems so lonely."

"Maybe we could find his parents," she said thoughtfully. "Do you think that would be the answer?"

"I don't know," replied David. "He seems–"

But they were interrupted by a terrible squealing noise from above.

"What's going on?" gasped Jenny, and they both ran out into the hall.

Auntie Joan came stumbling down the stairs, screaming, her face twisted in terror. Behind her buzzed the clockwork caterpillar, leaping from step to step, always just a few centimetres behind her.

"It's a madhouse up there," she said.

"Static electricity," her brother assured her, coming in from the shed. Directly he arrived at the foot of the stairs, the clockwork caterpillar was still.

"What's happened?" asked Mrs Golding. "I thought you were unpacking."

Auntie Joan sat down on the stairs, puffing and panting. "That little room. The one with the toys–"

"I told you about that," said Mrs Golding quickly. "They were left by the past owners and Reg won't disturb them."

"Disturb!" Auntie Joan repeated slowly. "What do you mean by disturb?"

"He won't move them," she said patiently. "We can't trace the last owner and–"

"The toys were moving."

"Moving?" Mrs Golding edged closer to Auntie Joan and Jenny wondered if she was trying to smell her breath. She'd overheard her mother telling her father that Auntie Joan had developed a drink problem.

"All over the place. I thought I saw someone, but I couldn't be sure. And there's a drawing pad up there. It says, 'Jack. Play with me'. Then it has Jenny and David's names. What does that mean?" But she didn't wait for an answer. "Directly I looked at the pad, the train started up, a ball bounced into me, a plane took off, a clockwork monkey started banging his drum, cars went in and out of a garage – and this, this *thing* chased me down the stairs."

David picked up the caterpillar. It had a cooling warmth, just like the cricket ball. He handed it to Jenny, who also felt its surface and then glanced back at him with a warning look.

"What does it mean?" asked Auntie Joan. "I'm coming over all faint."

Mr and Mrs Golding hauled her up, helped her into the living room and on to the sofa, where she lay reclining with a hastily poured glass of brandy.

"Maybe it's my nerves," she suggested.

"Yes, it must be," agreed Dad.

"I'll have a sleep," she said. "But you'll wake me for tea, won't you? I wouldn't want to miss that. Got to keep my strength up." Auntie Joan gave a brave little smile.

CHAPTER TWO

"I want to speak to you two," said their mother. "Now! In the kitchen."

David and Jenny trooped into the kitchen to find out what they had done. It was the Easter holidays and by tomorrow, their father said he would have finished repairing the old boat they had found moored up to their quay and it would be ready for a sail. Mr Golding had been working on the boat in any spare time he had from decorating the house and refurbishing the garden centre. He loved sailing.

"What have you two been up to?" Their mother stood in front of the kitchen table, her arms folded. "Come on!"

"Nothing," they chorused.

"I realise Auntie Joan has her problems, but she's Dad's sister and on her own. She deserves a little break, even if the house is in a shambles. But what she doesn't deserve – and can't take – is practical jokes being played on her."

"We didn't play any," said David indignantly.

"How did you move the toys? Strings? Wires?

And where did you hide? Our room's just below and–"

"Honestly, Mum," said Jenny. "We weren't even upstairs. We didn't do anything. It's her imagination."

"Yes," said David. "I reckon she's having a breakdown."

Their mother was suspicious, but in the end she had to accept denials with which she was clearly dissatisfied. Fortunately, nothing else happened all evening and the room upstairs was quiet during the night. Auntie Joan gradually recovered and was able to spend hours telling them all about her "troubles" – a long session only concluded when Mr Golding began to fall asleep at the table.

The shout of anger and the swearing began early the next morning. David ran to his bedroom window to see the postman reeling down the garden path, covered in what he thought at first was blue paint. Then he saw that it was ink. At his feet was a cricket ball.

David looked at his watch. Half-past seven and it was a Saturday. His mother was having a lie-in from the rigours of Auntie Joan, who was still asleep – he could hear her snoring. She always slept "deep", as she put it, but she also always denied snoring.

David decided he had better go down and see what had happened to the postman, although he was sure he knew. Jack, now activated, had been quiet for too long.

"What's up?"

"Did one of you kids do this?" asked the postman furiously.

"Of course we didn't."

"Then who did?"

David joined the postman on the steps. It was a windy morning, full of flurries of rain and fleeting sunshine. Looking up, David saw that Jack's window was open. He was sure that it had been closed yesterday and Dad had boarded up the broken pane.

Then David had a brainwave.

"It must have fallen," he said, pointing to the smashed bottle of ink lying on the ground near the cricket ball. "The window's open and it was on the ledge. The wind must have got round it somehow."

"That doesn't sound very likely," said the postman. He was still very angry.

"Do you want a wash?" asked David, trying to be as helpful as possible in the circumstances.

"I'm going back to the depot. Got an accident to report." The postman was still watching him suspiciously.

"What about the post?"

"Someone else will bring it out later. I'm in shock," he added. "Damn silly place to put a bottle of ink."

"We don't use that room," said David, by way of an excuse.

The postman bent down to examine the bottle. "Funny old-fashioned stuff. Haven't seen one of these around in years. You'd have thought it would have evaporated."

"That's right."

"I bent down to pick up this cricket ball. Looks too new to be lying around. I was just going to knock and hand it in when down comes the ink."

"How weird," said David. "But it must have been the wind. There couldn't be any other explanation." Jack obviously doesn't like the cricket ball being touched, he thought. I'd better take it up to him.

"Anyway, I'm off," said the postman, looking up at the open window as if more objects might come flying out – as well they might. "But you lot haven't heard the last of this." He walked away, glancing back several times over his shoulder, his blue-stained face catching the sunlight. It made him look like something from outer space.

David walked slowly up the creaking old stairs with the cricket ball in his hand. Even in daylight he felt uneasy about confronting Jack. He hadn't been afraid before, yet now he felt cold and apprehensive, despite the filtering sunlight on the stairs. The ball was cold in his hands, too – and getting colder all the time.

When he arrived at the attic, David saw there was a thin mist creeping out from under Jack's door, and when he tried to open it the handle was so cold that he let it go with a whimper.

"Jack," he called.

There was no reply but he thought he could detect a sigh.

"Jack?"

The door handle began to turn on its own.

CHAPTER THREE

The mist had almost vanished, and when David touched the brass handle again it was chilly but not nearly as cold as it had been.

Inside, the room was empty.

"Jack—"

Then David saw him, a dim, unfinished outline, crouched beneath the windowsill. He wore a T-shirt and jeans and an American baseball cap that was rammed hard down over his eyes.

"Jack? I brought you your cricket ball."

There was no reply.

"It was lying in the grass."

"Thanks." The voice was as thin as the mist.

David paused and then said abruptly, "Why did you throw that ink at the postman?"

"He hadn't brought a letter."

"What letter?"

"Saying where my parents are. Where they've moved to."

"Is your name Jack Fraser?"

"Yes. Do you know where they are?"

"No."

"You do." There was a threatening note in Jack's voice.

"I honestly don't. But I could try and find out for you."

"Liar."

"Look, Jack–"

He dodged just in time as the cricket ball hurtled past him.

"I don't know where they are," David gasped. "Why should I?"

The ball came again, narrowly missing him for the second time.

"You must do." Jack's misty eyes were full of an angry loneliness. "They sold you the house. They left me here."

David grabbed at the ball, but it was red hot again and he dropped it with a howl of anguish.

"What made you start up like this?" he asked wildly. "I mean – we've been here for six months and there hasn't been a peep out of you until now."

"I was waiting. Waiting to hear."

"Waiting to hear what?"

"Where my parents are. I was listening, but I didn't hear what I wanted." Jack sounded desperate, and despite the threat of the cricket ball and his increasing fear, David's heart went out to him.

"Let's talk. Stop trying to hit me with that ball."

But the door opened again and Jenny stood on the threshold. The cricket ball zoomed towards her.

Jenny caught it and threw it back hard, but the ball went through the window with a shattering of glass as she gave a howl of pain from its heat. Another pane gone. Both twins knew their parents would be furious.

"Now you've done it," said David.

"I don't care." She shook her fist at Jack's outline. "How dare you throw that ball at me? And what's that ink doing all over the grass?"

"It's all over the postman too," said David, and began to explain what had been happening.

When he had finished, Jack said, "I know you're lying to me. Both of you."

"We're not," said Jenny. "If you stop causing such a fuss, we'll try to help you."

"We didn't buy the house from your parents," David explained patiently. "The whole property belongs to Thames Garden Centres now. None of us here knows where your parents are – for the moment. But maybe we could find out."

"They left me behind," repeated Jack. "It's not fair." His outline was growing dimmer.

"You're fading away," said Jenny tenderly.

"I know. I can't help it." He sounded sulkily defiant.

"We'll help," promised David.

"You can start with Trent."

"Matthew Trent?" He was the handyman who helped Mr Golding with the garden centre.

"Yes, him."

"Did he know your parents?"

"He used to work here when my father owned the place. He'll know where they are." The engine on the model railway track started up and then came to a trickling halt, buzzing like a dying bee. "If you don't find them, I'll get you," Jack threatened, his voice light and drifting.

"You watch your lip," said David, "or you'll get nothing."

Their mother was thundering at the door now. "Did I hear a crash?" she demanded. "Did I hear the sound of breaking glass?"

"Er . . ."

Then she was on the threshold, her eyes accusing as she stared angrily at the latest broken pane.

"Another one gone?"

"I'm sorry, it was my fault," said David quickly. "The ball kind of slipped out of my hand. I don't know why but it's got a very greasy surface and I was just—"

"Playing catch up here? With a hard ball?" She gave him a look of withering contempt. "With all the work that Dad's got on – and with Auntie Joan downstairs, starting up those nerves of hers all over again—"

"We're sorry," said David and Jenny in unison.

"You should be. That's your pocket money gone for a month, David."

It's your fault, Jack, he thought as his mother ushered the twins downstairs to excited questions from Auntie Joan, which no one even attempted to answer.

"I've no idea where the Frasers are," said Matthew Trent, leaning grumpily on a spade while Mr Golding moved earth with a mechanical digger some metres away. He looked wary. "Why do you want to know?"

Trent was in his fifties, a grizzled and rather miserable man.

"We just thought you might," said Jenny. "Since you'd worked for them for so long."

"Well, I don't and that's that. We were never social, like."

"Why not?" asked David.

"Because they kept themselves to themselves – like I do. Too many nosy people about these days, young man. If you get my meaning."

But Jenny persisted. "It's just that we've almost got the boat ready to sail and we wondered if they'd like a photograph of her or anything. Dad says she's part of the estate – that the *Neptune* used to belong to the Frasers."

"That's right," he said abruptly.

"Wouldn't they want a photograph?"

"No." Trent stone-walled.

"Why not?"

"They'd want to forget the *Neptune*." He sounded very sure.

"Forget her?" Jenny continued to probe gently.

"Brought them bad luck, she did."

"How?"

"The boss spent too much time sailing – not enough on the business. I should know. I was the first to be laid off, wasn't I?" He sounded very aggrieved, but both David and Jenny could tell he was holding something back.

"She's a lovely sailing dinghy. No wonder they used her a lot," said David, anxious to keep him going.

Matthew Trent gazed around him at the big Victorian gabled house, the greenhouses, the sheds, the beds of flowers, the gravelled drive. "It's all coming shipshape now. Your dad's worth ten of that Fraser."

"What about Jack?" asked Jenny bluntly. "Did you know their son Jack?"

There was a veiled look in Trent's eyes now. "Jack," he repeated. "Selfish little– But then, so

24

was his dad. Always doing what they wanted to do. Hugo was never interested in running the garden centre. He was mad on sailing, but he was a real fantasy merchant, wasn't he?"

"What do you mean?" Jenny asked.

"Well – tiddly little craft like that. To hear him talk you'd have thought he was a transatlantic sailor, but all he ever did was to go up and down the river, just popping out to sea on a calm day. And Jack, he was always with him. That left Hilary and poor little Sally, his sister, to run this place. Of course Hugo went bust in the end."

"But all those toys," said Jenny. "Why did they leave all those toys in the room upstairs when they went? Did Dad tell you about that?" At last, she felt she was getting somewhere.

"Yeah. He told me. But I'm not surprised they left them, like."

"Not surprised?"

Trent returned to his digging. He didn't seem to want to say any more.

"Please tell us why." Jenny was at her most persuasive.

"I don't think your dad–"

"He won't mind," said David reassuringly, knowing he probably would, particularly as he had kept the secret from them so far.

"Jack drowned."

The statement was bleak.

"Drowned?" David repeated. "How?"

"Fell out of the *Neptune*, didn't he? They recovered his body but of course it was too late. Everything slid away after Jack died. He may have been selfish like his dad, but he was much loved by his mum and his sister. No one had the heart to fight for the business any longer, so they gradually let it go bust and then they left. I suppose they couldn't bear to take any of the toys or the other bits and pieces in Jack's room. So now you know," Trent finished aggressively. "But don't you two let on to your dad I told you – or your mum. I don't want to lose me job again."

"We won't," said Jenny, anxious to reassure him.

"What are we going to do?" asked David as they walked down to the water's edge and the rusty old quayside where the *Neptune* was moored. The little boat bobbed up and down in the strong tide, its tattered pennant flying in the wind, with a new coat of varnish and the name carefully picked out in red paint on the side.

"Find the Frasers. Jack's trapped in that room. We could go to the Thames Garden Centres office and–" Jenny was all enthusiasm.

"I'm not sure they'll give us the details," said

David uneasily. "Why should they? A couple of kids? And I don't think either Mum or Dad'll be much help. They won't exactly buy the idea of a poltergeist boy lurking in an upstairs room, throwing cricket balls at us and sending clockwork caterpillars after Auntie Joan. They might find all that too hard to swallow, don't you think?"

"Yes, probably," replied Jenny. "But it's still up to us, isn't it? Someone's got to help poor Jack."

"I'm not sure I like him," said David reflectively.

"He's only mean because he's trapped in that room. He should be with his parents." Jenny was briskly kind.

"Perhaps they don't want him," replied her brother.

CHAPTER FOUR

"Yuk!" Matthew Trent was standing in the drive by the house, covered in something liquid and sticky, most of which was still pouring down him.

"What's happened?" asked David as the twins ran towards him, certain that Jack must be up to his tricks again.

"I was standing down here, minding my own business, when I got properly soaked. I don't know who's up there playing funny–" He was looking at both of them with mounting suspicion, but he was more shocked than angry.

"Well, it can't have been us," said David. "We were down by the river, looking at the *Neptune*."

"You could have doubled back," said Matthew Trent.

"Don't be daft." Jenny was angry. "How could we have done that?" It was all too much. Jack was really going to get them into trouble this time.

"You're fast on your feet–"

"Not that fast," said David. "We'd have had to

28

go at the speed of light to get up into the attic and start chucking things at you."

"Funny," Trent said absently, licking his lips and losing his indignation for a moment as a faraway look came into his eyes.

"Now what?" Jenny was still furious.

"This tastes of home-made ginger beer. Flat, gone-off ginger beer."

"What's home-made ginger beer?" asked David.

"It's a drink that was around a lot a dozen or more years ago. I used to rather fancy it." He licked his lips again, almost appreciatively. "But what I don't like is having the stuff thrown all over me as some kind of joke."

"What's this about a joke?" asked Mrs Golding grimly, coming out of the house at just the wrong moment.

"Someone threw ginger beer all over me," said Matthew Trent indignantly.

"Where from?" she asked, eyeing the twins even more grimly.

"Up there. The window that's been broken a couple of times." He turned round to raise a horny finger, pointing up at Jack's room. "It's open. See."

"Well?" asked Mum. "Which of you twins played this stupid trick? Or was it both of you?"

"It wasn't either of us, Mum," said Jenny.

"Then who was it? Me? Your dad? Auntie Joan?"

"Maybe she did do it," David speculated. "You know she's off her trolley."

"Right," said their mother. "That's it. Why are you both lying to me?"

"We're not," said Jenny. "We were down by the river when Mr Trent got showered with ginger beer. We weren't anywhere near that window."

Mrs Golding turned to Matthew Trent, looking a little less agitated. "I must admit Jenny never lies."

"Neither do I," protested David hotly.

"No, dear. You just bend the truth a little."

"I always–"

"Shut up, David!" their mother yelled just as Auntie Joan came pottering along, looking for a sunny place where she could sit down and do some knitting.

"Is there trouble?" she asked eagerly. "Someone done something wrong?"

"No," said Mrs Golding. "We're just having a friendly chat, that's all."

David and Jenny reluctantly followed their mother inside, leaving Auntie Joan and Matthew Trent locked in an impossible conversation the twins could hear through the open door.

"You seem to be very sticky, Mr Trant," Auntie Joan was saying.

"Trent, madam. I believe it's home-made ginger beer."

"I remember that. Such a lovely drink! Did your hand shake?"

"Shake?"

"When you were drinking, Mr Trant. You seem to have thrown your ginger beer over yourself."

"It was dropped, madam."

"Dropped? What do you mean, dropped?"

"Dropped from a great height."

"Who by?"

Mercifully their voices faded at the head of the stairs.

The empty ginger-beer bottle lay on the floor.

"Now come on, it's all well past a joke," said Mum. "Tell me what happened."

"I didn't do it, Mum. I swear." Jenny was adamant.

"Neither did I," David repeated.

"Look, I don't want to—" But their mother's attempts at investigation were drowned by their father's voice.

"Who's for a sail after lunch?" He was coming

up the stairs to find his family. "What are you doing here?"

"*You* might be going on the water," said his wife, "but they're not."

"Why?" asked Dad in astonishment.

But before they could say anything, she screamed.

The clockwork spider, black and hairy with eyes on stalks that were even now revolving, lurched its way towards Mum and began to climb over her foot. She screamed again.

"It's only clockwork," said Dad.

"Take it away!"

Mr Golding bent down, picked up the spider and immediately dropped it with a cry of pain. "It's red hot," he gasped.

David was quick to catch the cricket ball, which hurtled from a corner and would have hit his father's head, had he not intercepted it. David tossed the ball from hand to hand until it began to cool down.

"You see – we didn't do anything."

Their mother watched the slowly winding-down clockwork spider in horrible fascination. "I just don't get this."

As Mr and Mrs Golding examined the toy, Jenny grabbed David's arm and pointed to the pad

David had written their names on. A Biro was scribbling on it.

IT'S MY BOAT. KEEP OFF.

Rapidly, Jenny wrote, WHY ARE YOU SO SELFISH?

"I'm confiscating this ball," muttered David, shoving it in his pocket. "It's lethal."

"There's only one answer," said their father at last.

"Static electricity?" the twins chorused.

"Yes. How did you know?"

"I apologise to both of you." Mrs Golding was always scrupulously fair.

The wooden bricks rose slowly and began to pelt them.

"What's that?" Dad ducked and the bricks passed over his head.

"Call that static electricity?" asked Mrs Golding.

"Air currents," he muttered. "Rising hot air. Could be affecting all the wiring."

The bricks clattered to the floor as Mr Golding opened a fuse box on the wall. Meanwhile Jack's Biro wrote on the pad, YOU'RE NOT TO GO ON MY BOAT.

"Behave yourself," whispered David, "or you'll get done over. Somehow."

A very rude word appeared but the twins ignored Jack's fury, turning their backs on him while their parents were still examining the fuse box. As they watched, they were both very tense, expecting something to hit them, but nothing happened.

"Look at this," said Mr Golding.

"What about it?" Mum was suspicious.

"The fuses – they're burnt out. There must have been a powerful surge of electricity in this room – so powerful it could move objects."

David knew his father believed in what he was saying – he was reaching out for an explanation and grimly sticking to it, as he often did. But would Mum go along with him?

"Oh, well." She was wavering. "If you're right, what are we going to do about it? Get the electricity people in?"

Mr Golding shook his head. "I want the room closed until things have settled down. I'll have a word with a mate of mine who's in the electricity line."

The vague explanation almost set Mrs Golding off again, but suddenly she gave in. Maybe she was too exhausted to continue, thought Jenny.

"All right then." She turned reluctantly to the twins. "I don't understand any of this so I'm going to give you the benefit of the doubt. But you're not to come up here again. Is that clear?"

They both nodded, and then David asked tentatively, "Can we go out with Dad in the *Neptune* – since we're not to blame any more?"

"I didn't say that," their mother snapped. "I said I didn't understand it, that's all. I'm still trying to get to the bottom of it, but if I discover–" She broke off, looking at the hopeful expressions of her husband and children. "All right."

"Would you like to come, Mum?" asked Jenny, although she knew her mother disliked the water. It would be good, she thought, if the *Neptune*'s first voyage with her new family also gave Mum some confidence. But Mrs Golding wouldn't hear of it.

"Go on – all three of you. Take the thing out after lunch. Auntie Joan and I could do with some peace."

Jack's pen began to scribble again on the pad, and as the twins left the room they saw he had written in block capitals, IF YOU GO OUT IN MY BOAT, I'LL SEE YOU GET INTO REAL TROUBLE.

"I wonder what he means by *real* trouble," whispered Jenny.

"He can't really do anything much," David scoffed.

Jack's laughter was both mocking and angry, but the twins noticed to their relief that their parents hadn't heard a sound.

A shiver of fear went through David. Somehow, Jack seemed rather more menacing now.

CHAPTER FIVE

Jack was outraged at their planned use of the *Neptune*. Merely throwing objects around the room and out of the window was no longer enough for him.

The Goldings were just finishing lunch when Matthew Trent arrived, looking wild-eyed. Sweat stood out on his forehead and one of his hands was trembling so much that he clasped it in the other. "I don't get it," he said repeatedly. "I just don't get it."

"What is it?" asked Mrs Golding. "What's gone wrong now?"

Auntie Joan gave a little groan and clasped a hand to her heart, but from the eager look in her eyes, Jenny knew that the old lady was eagerly anticipating the latest disaster.

"The new fencing we put up by the river–" Trent began.

"Yes?" prompted Mr Golding nervously.

"It's lying in the mud."

"I suppose it must have blown down," suggested Mrs Golding.

"There's not nearly enough wind for that," Trent said indignantly. "And besides, there's a couple of garden gnomes gone in as well."

"Fresh wind?" asked Dad, again searching for a rational explanation.

"More like vandalism," said Mrs Golding.

It was extraordinary, thought David, how much adults were prepared to block their minds and make up so-called reasonable explanations for the inexplicable.

"Vandals," breathed Auntie Joan in excitement. "They're all over the country. Crawling round every street corner."

"Crawling?" asked David, but already the others were on their feet, heading for the quay.

"Vandals,"repeated Auntie Joan. "The scourge of the nation."

But Jenny and David knew there was only one vandal involved. Jack. Poltergeist Jack.

Matthew Trent had not been exaggerating. Two sections of strong pale fencing were stretched out on the mud and two garden gnomes lay on their backs as if sunbathing. The Thames water lapped a few metres away.

"Did you see anyone?" asked Auntie Joan fever-ishly, darting glances around the foreshore as if she thought vandals might be lurking there. But there was nobody.

"No," replied Trent shortly. "We'd best be getting that stuff out of the mud before the tide comes in." He gave Auntie Joan a quizzical look. "It's a gumboots job."

"I don't think I'm quite up to–" she began.

Mrs Golding quickly came to her rescue. "Of course you're not, dear."

"It's just that my sense of balance isn't what it used to be."

David had the sudden image of Auntie Joan upside-down in the mud, and grinned. Mum, catching the grin, frowned at him.

"We'll manage," she said. "Let's get our boots on. The job won't take long with five of us."

But it took a great deal longer than expected because the mud was deep, and where it wasn't deep it was slippery. They all fell into the sludge more than once. David was sure he could hear mocking laughter coming from the house.

"I'll get him," he promised Jenny. "I'll really get him for this."

"I don't see why boys always think they can work things out with violence," his twin said irritably as she slid across the mud, pulling a gnome behind her. "Besides, you can't thump a ghost."

"I'll pay him out," muttered David as he lost his grip on the other gnome and fell over – on his back this time. He got up, spluttering, but immediately slipped over again.

"You're changing colour," said Jenny, exploding with laughter, while her parents and Matthew Trent battled with the fencing. "Not brown but black. Very black."

"Why don't you push off!" shouted David, struggling to his feet, the mud yielding him up with a horrible sucking sound.

"That's just what you're doing to that gnome," pointed out Jenny. "He's almost in the water."

"Dave! What are you doing?" bellowed his father. "You're meant to be rescuing them – not launching them."

With a strangled cry of rage, David squelched knee-deep into a particularly soft patch of mud. The laughter from the house seemed to grow even louder, but Jenny now knew for a certainty that only she and David could hear it.

After they had all had showers, Jenny, David and their father clambered on board the *Neptune*. Once they had cast off, the rising tide soon edged her away from the wharf. She tacked across the river, her sail fluttering and then filling in the strengthening breeze. Mr Golding had been a keen sailor when he was younger, and all three of them had been on a sailing course the previous summer. However, they soon discovered that the *Neptune* seemed to have a life of her own. She was slow to respond and the boom swung unpredictably. Of course, the twins assured one another, it must be the wind.

Jenny was at the helm and David and their father sat on either side of the *Neptune*, adjusting their weight to the wind. As she sailed on erratically, they began to feel they were getting used to her.

It was a Saturday afternoon and there wasn't much movement on the river. The long barges weren't operating, and only the odd tug or two stirred up enough wake to send the *Neptune* wallowing. This part of the river had once been docks and industry, but all that had long since died away, leaving vast areas of derelict wharves and the slow rise of office and apartment blocks.

"Let's head for the old dockyard," said David.

"Can we tie up there?" asked Jenny. "We could go into that old abandoned bit – you know, with all the graffiti going back centuries."

"OK," said Mr Golding happily.

The slapping of sail, the bouncing tide and the light, sparkling sunshine overhead banished Jack from the minds of Jenny and David and also seemed to soothe away their father's worries about the slow progress towards the opening of the garden centre.

The area where Jenny wanted to land was a collection of mouldering old warehouses, the brickwork of which was inscribed with names and messages from workers over hundreds of years. In the centre of the buildings was a cobbled square. The atmosphere always pulled Jenny back into the past, and because she knew that the museum was shortly due to take over the site, she reckoned this might be their last chance of being there alone, with the sea birds calling hauntingly above them.

The boom swung wildly again and Mr Golding and David ducked quickly.

"Sorry," said Jenny. They were on a run now but she hadn't detected any change in the wind direction. "I didn't expect that."

"Neither did I," said their father, gazing in puzzlement at the tattered pennant.

"Maybe it's the wharves," suggested David. "They might break the wind up."

"Maybe," said Jenny doubtfully.

Then the boom came over again, as suddenly and as viciously as the flight of a cricket ball. Cricket ball, Jenny wondered and she caught David's eye. He nodded, and his hand went to his anorak pocket in pain and alarm. She knew what was happening. Just to complicate things, the ball was getting hot again.

David pulled it out and placed it in the scuppers.

"Why have you brought that thing?" asked his father.

"Thought I might have a chance to practise a bit," he said quickly.

Jenny knew that David hadn't wanted to leave the ball behind in case it hurt their mother – or even Auntie Joan or Matthew Trent – but could Jack be messing about with the boom? The thought made her feel very uneasy.

CHAPTER SIX

The warehouses loomed up at them, their dark, crumbling shapes caught by the sun, making them look like an ancient city, deserted by its inhabitants. Jenny and her father got the *Neptune*'s sails down without incident, but as David tried to moor the craft to an iron ring, the dinghy was thrown against the weed-covered wharf with such force that Jenny lost her footing and collapsed in the stern and David almost got his fingers crushed.

"You two OK?" Their father was still precariously on his feet.

"Just about," said Jenny, struggling up.

"Weird," replied David, looking flustered. "There weren't any other boats – no wash, nothing. Yet we got slammed against the side."

For once their father had no immediate answer. There was a short silence and then he said, "I'm not sure we should land."

They could see that he was uneasy and at a loss for a rational explanation of what had happened.

Jenny was immediately indignant. "Not land? I want to go and have a look at the graffiti."

"The museum may have taken over by now," their father replied. "We might be trespassing."

"Can't see a sign," persisted Jenny doggedly.

Mr Golding scanned the foreshore. Then he said warily, "OK – but we mustn't be too long."

When they had disembarked, David glanced back at the *Neptune*, bobbing up and down on the tide. She looked innocent enough but with Jack around . . . Suddenly he dreaded the homeward voyage.

The trio kept close together, with Jenny slightly in the lead, as they walked over the cobbles into the dark passageways between the buildings. Here and there, a sunbeam penetrated from a sky that had a pale sun and increasingly swollen rain clouds; once it picked out a rat running for cover and David shuddered. Why did Jenny like this foul place, abandoned so long ago? Even his father seemed apprehensive, continually peering into the shadows.

They walked on into the central square, which had piles of ropes and tarpaulins and a cement mixer looking forlorn and out of place.

"The restoration's going to begin soon," said Mr Golding, but David and Jenny only grunted.

45

David was feeling more and more certain that something was going to happen, and Jenny was sorry that the chattering public would soon be milling around her ghost town.

David glanced back again, convinced he had seen someone duck back behind the last corner. A wind whistled along the cobbles, whisking up a paper bag and sending it sliding towards them. A broom fell from its position against the long wooden sheds where ropes had once been made, and a half-open door blew shut, making them all jump.

"Best get some shelter," said their father, walking faster. "There's a squall coming up."

Darkening rain lashed the cobbles as they sheltered in a doorway. They had arrived at the entrance to the old dormitories, where prisoners working in the dockyard had slept, or maybe, as Jenny thought, were too tired to sleep properly and lay awake, dreading the hardships of the next day.

Opposite them, in the centre of the cobbled square, was an old well, sealed by a slatted wooden cover. Seconds later, David saw it fly off.

"Wind's taken that," said their father.

Jenny looked sharply at David. She knew they

were both thinking the same thing; it was as if someone had pushed the cover up from underneath.

The rain lashed again and then grew lighter as the wind died, and they were left in silence except for the running of water over the cobbles.

"Don't like the look of that sky,"said their father. "We'd better stay here for a while."

"I'm just going to take a look at that well," said Jenny. "Shan't be a sec."

She was off before either her father or brother could try to stop her.

The wind returned as she ran across the square and almost seemed to blow her towards the well. As she passed the mildewed but heavy wooden cover, Jenny felt a stab of fear and realised that she should never have left the others. She glanced back and saw David and her father standing in the shadow of the dormitory, looking remote and frighteningly beyond her reach.

Reluctantly she continued, the wind dropping marginally, but Jenny could almost feel it waiting for her, ready to spring. She imagined it coiled, shuddering with airy laughter.

At last she was standing by the well and cautiously looking down into its depths. Was that water lapping? She picked up a stone and threw it in. A very long time seemed to pass before Jenny heard the light plop.

She could make out a faint glow. Was something phosphorous down there? The glow became brighter, spreading into a circle, into a face. Into Jack's face.

He was gazing up at her, shimmering down there, his tongue poking out at her. Then he began to call mockingly, gurgling as if his mouth was full of water.

"I drowned, Jenny," he said. "I drowned."

At first she was too frightened to reply. Then she forced herself to say, "Jack? Is that you, Jack?"

"It's me, Jenny."

"I – we want to help you."

"I don't believe you." The gurgling voice was childishly spiteful. "You've never been helpful."

"We *want* to be. But we don't know what to do."

"You said you'd find my parents."

"We're trying," she pleaded.

"No, you're not," he said accusingly. "You've stolen my boat instead."

"We didn't mean to. Tomorrow, we'll try to find out more about your parents. I promise."

"I don't trust you."

"You have to try."

48

"I'll never trust you." And Jack blew a great spout of stinking water up at her.

Jenny staggered back from the well. The stagnant liquid was foul-smelling and acrid. But the attack made her angry.

She returned to the well and stared down into the dark water. There was no glint of phosphorus this time and nothing moved.

"You watch it, Jack Fraser," she whispered. "Silly boys who play tricks don't get any help at all."

There was silence except for a strange croaking sound, and when Jenny drew back from the mouth of the well she saw a large toad squatting below her. Then the creature slowly hopped away.

Mr Golding had strolled off to look more closely at the graffiti, so Jenny could tell David what Jack had done.

"I can smell that water," he said unhelpfully when she had finished. "It really stinks."

"Thanks a lot," she replied miserably.

"Jack's gone too far," he added hastily. To David, spitting dirty water was more of a joke than anything else. It was what the poltergeist could do to them on the river that really made him afraid. "Let's take a look at the graffiti," he said. "And then we'll sail back. Looks like the weather's getting brighter."

It was. The watery sun had returned and the wind was dropping as the twins wandered over to their father and then on to another wall to read the scratched and carved scribblings. JAMES DOWDEN, 1872. I WORKED HERE -- ARTHUR SEAFIELD, 1709. IN THE NAME OF THE LORD, GRANT ME PEACE. ISAIAH HUMBLEWEED, 1744. I COMMEND MYSELF TO THE GOOD GOD. ALBERT HAMMEND, 1814.

David suddenly stepped back, giving a little gasp of fear, and Jenny hurried over to him. In a heavy metal box were a number of tins of white paint and a couple of new brushes. One tin was open – and a brush was travelling towards it.

The twins watched in amazement as the brush flew to the wall and began to write, GIVE ME BACK MY BOAT. IT DOESN´T BELONG TO YOU. There was a pause while it hovered uncertainly in mid-air. Then it wrote abruptly, GIVE ME BACK MY SISTER.

"Sister?" whispered David. "Whose sister?"

"Jack's, of course. Who else could be writing this?" said Jenny impatiently.

"But why should he think we've taken his sister?"

"Maybe she's got something to do with the *Neptune*," replied Jenny. Then she yelled, "Watch out!" The brush spun round in mid-air and headed for David. He ducked and it flew over his head, landing on the cobbles. Then the paint tin rose and came towards him as well.

CHAPTER SEVEN

"David!" Jenny shouted, but the tin had altered direction, moving towards her at considerable speed, with the paint slopping over the sides. She ducked, she ran, and then threw herself flat on the cobbles. Jack was fooled and the tin went flying over her head, crashing to the ground just behind the well, spreading a white lake over the rain-washed cobbles.

Jenny got up and waved her fist in the air. "And you want our help?" she yelled. "You must be crazy!"

"You two OK?" asked Mr Golding as he returned from an inspection of the old boiler room.

"We were playing a game," said David.

"Yes?" But his interest was elsewhere. "I hope they're going to preserve some of that machinery in there. I saw a winch motor that could still be made to work. I wouldn't mind coming back when the museum's got going and having a look at what they've done. You sure you two are OK? You both look as if you've seen a ghost. And what's that paint all over the cobbles?"

52

"We–" David began, but his father was looking up at the sky.

"Let's set sail before that wind comes back."

At first David thought everything was going to be all right, and so did Jenny. Their father was more relaxed as the *Neptune* slipped away from her mooring into a calm, silky sheet of water, but as she reached the centre of the river, they saw a huge purple-black cloud in the distance, and the water turned as dark as the passageways between the warehouses.

For a while, with David at the helm, the *Neptune* tacked to and fro in a dead calm, the sail slack and only the tide gradually taking her upriver. There was a laziness to the Thames, as if it was preparing itself unwillingly for trouble to come. Then there was a distant growl of thunder and soon a series of ear-splitting cracks.

High wharves loomed on either side as, with an even louder crack of thunder, the wind came screaming in like a banshee, howling among the derelict buildings, screeching through open roofs and glassless windows and whipping up the surface of the river, sending waves scudding erratically to and fro.

"We've got to land," shouted their father above

the wailing elements, but neither Jenny nor David could see a single possible landing place.

"Let's get the sail down," yelled Jenny. "She won't take all this."

David tried to manoeuvre the *Neptune* out of the direct blast of the wind as Jenny and their father began to pull down the wildly flapping sail. It was a slow and difficult job. As Jenny pulled the last of the canvas down on to the deck, she saw some initials carved into the mast which she had not spotted before. J.F. Jack Fraser.

Just as she had identified them, she heard David shouting. Looking up, Jenny saw the boom coming towards her so fast that she had no chance of getting out of the way. She tried to duck, but it hit her on the side of the head and pitched her into the waves.

David saw his sister floating on her back in her life jacket. Unconscious, she was being carried away from the *Neptune*. Knowing that he was a strong swimmer and his father wasn't, David yelled, "I'll go after her! Try and steer the boat towards us."

His father nodded, but they both realised that the *Neptune* was now only running on her foresail and she would be hard to steer. The wind showed no sign of abating, and as David went backwards over the bow, the rain lashed the river. The waves seemed bigger than ever, and there was a swell that made the water surge, tide versus wind, with the wind getting the upper hand.

David struck out but instantly felt the pull. Seeing Jenny still on her back, he swam harder, pushing himself far beyond what he thought he was capable of. Several times he glanced back towards the *Neptune*, which was kept more or less stationary by the wind and the tide.

Fear stabbed at the back of his consciousness, but was overwhelmed by the sheer physical effort. As he saw he was gradually nearing Jenny, David briefly felt more optimistic. He had qualified in life-saving at school, but he was not sure that he would have the strength to bring her back to the *Neptune*. And there was no other vessel in sight.

Forcing the panic out of his mind, David swam on. He couldn't afford to think ahead now – he knew he just had to keep going.

At last, swallowing oily water, he reached her. Turning on his back, he pulled Jenny into the life-saving position.

"Can you hear me?" he gasped.

There was no response.

"Can you hear me, Jenny?"

"Yes." Her voice was faint.

"Just relax. I'm taking you back to the *Neptune*."

He thought she was going out again, but struggled on. For all his efforts, he was making practically no progress at all. Desperately, David tried to calm himself, but when he looked back at the *Neptune* he saw she was still a long way off. The panic welled up and spread inside him, making him gulp in more water.

"Sister," came the voice. "You've got to get my sister."

Now, another tousled, dripping head was next to his in the trough of a wave. "Sister," the voice said again. 'Sister."

"Help me," spluttered David. "You've got to help me, Jack."

"You took my boat."

"Please!"

"Sister drowned."

"So will mine if you don't help."

"Don't care."

"You *must* care."

David struggled on alone. How could Jack help him anyway?

He knew he wasn't going to make it now. Jenny was a dead weight and the tide was taking him away from the *Neptune* rather than towards it. The rain had lessened, but the wind had increased and the waves kept closing over his head. Somehow David just managed to keep a grip on Jenny, but she, like the waves, was weighing him down, pushing him under the freezing water.

Peering anxiously behind him, David thought the *Neptune* was a little closer, but there was still a vast stretch between him and safety. Slowly, he lost not only strength but will, and he wondered what it would be like to drown. Maybe it would be easier just to slip under the waves and give up.

"Don't give up."

What was that, David wondered. A voice? A thought? A dream? He was hazy now, and he could feel Jenny slipping out of his hands. Nothing mattered.

"David! Don't give up." The voice was urgent, commanding, breaking through his need to let go. He felt Jenny lifting, the weight decreasing, the hopelessness fading. Suddenly, David realised that they were making progress and the *Neptune* was coming wonderfully, gloriously nearer.

David saw Jack's head beside his own, the strong arms and the thrashing legs sending the water churning away behind him, making the impossible rescue possible after all. Already he was feeling stronger, and it wasn't long before he was bumped by the bow of the *Neptune*. He was hazily aware of his father lifting Jenny carefully, almost effortlessly, into the wildly swaying boat. For a moment David was terrified it would capsize, but, amazingly, it stayed upright as he felt himself dragged gently over the bow.

"Jenny's fine," said his father, helming the *Neptune* up the river with the foresail now full and the wind lighter. Now it seemed to be blowing in one direction and the boat was slowly making a course for home.

"Just had a knock on the head, no more. I'll get the hospital to take a look but she's conscious now."

Jenny was pale. "Who pulled me out?" she asked.

"David did," Dad replied. "He's a real hero. I thought for a moment he was in trouble, but then he picked up again." His voice shook and the twins knew how afraid he had been. "Then David didn't let up until he got you back to me. Amazing."

Jenny looked at her brother intently and muttered the word, "How?"

David whispered, "Jack," and then, to make sure she understood, whispered again, "He helped me."

"What are you going to do? asked Jenny, her voice strengthening. "Call an ambulance? I don't want to go to hospital. Honestly, Dad, I'll be fine once I've warmed up."

"You took a nasty crack on the head and you can never be sure about concussion. Do you feel sleepy?"

"That's the last thing I feel," she asserted.

But her father was adamant. "I'll drive you there in the car and wait with you. We can't take any risks."

As their own familiar wharf loomed up, David felt completely bewildered. Why had Jack helped him? And what was the poltergeist going to do next?

CHAPTER EIGHT

David decided not to go along to the hospital but to stay at home in the hope of being able to talk to Matthew Trent. He was sure he could tell him more about the Frasers, and not only help them to understand about Jack's sister but also give them some clues to the family's possible whereabouts.

Unfortunately, before he could approach Trent, David had to tell the full story of the so-called sailing accident to his mother, with Auntie Joan listening avidly. It was only after a long argument that David was able to get her to agree to a "quiet evening watching TV" rather than immediately going to bed.

"That boat," Mum began again. "I told your father he should never have rebuilt the thing or taken you out on the river. It's far, far too–"

"Honestly, Mum, you know we took that sailing course and–"

In the end she quietened down, mainly because Auntie Joan kept chiming in and interfering. "Well, don't let's overlook the fact that you're a hero," said his mother, guiltily switching from condemnation to praise. "I'll never forget you saved Jenny's life. I'm *so* proud of you."

David, taken aback by this sudden reversal, was unable to dodge several smacking kisses.

Auntie Joan said, "I'm going to ring the newspapers. I'll get on to the *Sun*—" She was wild with excitement.

"Oh no you won't," said Mum. "I'm not having that lot down here."

"The boy deserves a medal. Would you prefer the *Mail*?" she asked more genteelly.

"I'd prefer nothing!" Mrs Golding replied, forgetting how easy it was to offend Auntie Joan, who got up immediately with a pained expression on her face.

"I see. Well, I was only trying to help. But obviously it's not wanted. I'll go to my room."

"Joan! Don't take on like that. I only meant—"

But she was already marching out of the room, working herself up into a mood and muttering, "I know I'm not welcome here . . ."

"Joan!" Mrs Golding plunged after her, pursuing her up the stairs, while David grinned. This would give him the opportunity to duck out and try to grab Matthew Trent before he left for the night. He heard the satisfying slam of Auntie Joan's bedroom door and his mother pounding on it. David stole out, knowing she would definitely be occupied for some time.

"Mr Trent?"

"I hear you're a hero." For once he was affable.

"I only–"

"Good on you, son. I love to see someone with some guts. I'm sure your sister will be fine."

"I've been wondering . . ."

"Wondering?"

"About the Frasers."

"Now why are you so concerned about them?" The suspicion was back.

"Jenny saw their son had carved his initials on the mast of the *Neptune*. Was it his boat?"

"He did most of the sailing," said Trent reluctantly.

"And his sister? Was she drowned?"

"No, she survived. It was Jack who drowned, saving her."

"Why didn't you tell me?" David asked indignantly.

"Thought it might put you off the boat. I like to see it being sailed – although I'm sorry about the accident." Matthew Trent was very uneasy.

"So Jack wasn't that selfish."

"Not in the end."

"And you've no idea where the family is now?"

"No."

"Or the sister?"

There was a long silence. Then Trent began hesitantly, "Sally. The daughter. I thought I saw her last year. But I could be wrong. It looked like her, though – working in the Chinese take-away. The Three Kingdoms, it's called."

"Did she recognise you?"

"If she did, she didn't show it. But Sally was only young when it all happened. Now she would be in her early twenties and I've aged a bit since then."

"Has she got any distinctive features?" asked David.

"Yes. She had thick blonde hair and she used to have this angelic face. I suppose she still does in a way, except that it's matured a bit, like. But I could be wrong and most likely am." Matthew Trent looked as if he wanted to end the conversation there.

"Why didn't you tell us all this before?" David repeated.

Matthew Trent looked uncomfortable. "It was all a long time ago," he said evasively.

"Is that the only reason?" He was sure it wasn't.

There was no reply.

David persevered. "I do want to know. We both do. I suppose it's to do with the *Neptune*. We inherited her – and with boats you can sometimes feel something about their last owners."

That was as far as he was prepared to go, but it had a considerable effect on Matthew Trent, who seemed to relax as if suddenly reassured.

"Funny you should say that. You can feel other people in things – in objects. I'm no sailor, but as I go round the old buildings here, I can remember the Frasers. They were like my own family in a a way. A special way." He paused and David waited for him to continue. "I was in a children's home mostly when I was a kid, and then I went into a hostel. I did a load of dud jobs and then came here and I was with the Frasers for about fifteen years – fifteen good years. Jack was born and then Sally. When I had to leave I was devastated – couldn't cope. I got myself a room and grieved for them as I picked up one bum job after another. Went on for years. Then, just because I still hung around, your dad took me on again, let me help to get the old place back to what it was. But I didn't want to tell you about Jack, let alone Sally."

"Why not?" asked David gently.

"I guess I'm kind of superstitious . . ."

David waited, wondering if Matthew Trent had also seen Jack or sensed his misery.

"I thought if I got too friendly – started confiding – then I'd be in trouble."

"You're not," said David, "and we're not going bankrupt either. Dad's only the manager and I'm sure the company want this place to pay. They wouldn't be putting so much money into it if they didn't." He paused, and then added, "My dad will make a go of this. He'll make a go of it with you. Jenny and I like you, Mr Trent. We like you a lot."

Matthew Trent gazed at him searchingly and then smiled. "Call me Matt," he said.

David went back inside the house, knowing that at last he had made a little progress. He also knew that he needed not only to communicate this to Jack at once but also to thank him for saving Jenny – just as he had saved Sally. Stealing into the hallway, David heard the TV and saw his mother slumped in front of it, eating chocolates, something she only did when she was fed up or under pressure. Evidently Auntie Joan was still up in her room.

"OK, Mum?"

She looked up, her face drawn and tired. "I had a call from your dad. Jenny's fine, but they're going to keep her in overnight just in case, and your dad's staying with her. She'll be discharged tomorrow morning."

David went over and kissed her on the forehead. "You look done in."

"Where have you been?" she asked weakly. "You should be resting."

"I was talking to Matthew Trent. I like him."

"Yes. So do I."

"We will keep him on, Mum, won't we?"

"I'm sure we will. We could do with another two of him."

"He's lonely."

"I sensed that," said Mrs Golding. "Don't worry – there's room for him here. I think he feels he's come home."

"I'm just going upstairs. Then I'll sit with you for a bit."

"What do you want up there?" she asked suspiciously.

"Just a tissue."

"You're getting a cold–" she began.

David changed the subject fast. "Where's Auntie Joan?"

"She's taken offence. Locked herself in her room."

"That's nothing unusual."

His mother laughed and then looked worried again. "It's been such a shock. Jenny could have drowned."

"No, she wouldn't." David could see that she

needed reassuring. "Don't exaggerate it, Mum. She wasn't that far from the boat and I had a grip on her all the time."

"I don't want you using that *Neptune*."

"Mum!"

"There's something wrong with it."

"There's nothing wrong with it. We ran into a squall, that's all."

But she didn't seem to hear him. "You don't know where that boat's been," she said unexpectedly. "You don't know who had it last."

"The Frasers," replied David. "Have you been talking to Matthew?"

"He told me all about that poor boy – and the little girl going overboard."

"So you do know."

She nodded. "It could have been Jenny – or you."

"Well, it wasn't," said David firmly.

"That Matthew – I told him not to tell you or Jenny anything about what happened."

"I forced it out of him."

"How?"

"There's some initials carved on the mast. J.F. I had to know, Mum."

"And he told you?"

"Don't blame him," insisted David. "Don't blame Matt."

She sighed and wiped away a tear. "I won't," she said. "But I wish we'd never come here."

How much had she guessed, David wondered. What vibrations had his mother picked up? But the last thing he wanted to do was to try and find out. Jack wouldn't wait, and unless he tried to pacify him, matters might get much worse. If that was possible.

Slowly and apprehensively David opened Jack's door. The room was full of the jumbled toys and books, the divan and chest of drawers, the football posters on the walls – but there was no sign of the poltergeist.

Then something hit him hard behind the ear and he went down on the floor.

"Get up," said a familiar voice. "Get up and fight."

Two boxing gloves were hovering in the air and they looked as if they meant business.

"I had lessons," said Jack. "Boxing lessons."

"I didn't," said David unhappily. "I came up here to thank you, not to fight."

"You think I'm soft?"

"Soft? Why?"

"I helped you."

"That's why I came to thank you." David was desperate.

"I helped my sister too. But I can't remember what happened after that."

"You drowned," said David. "You drowned dead."

"I'm not dead." Jack's voice rose in anger. "My parents went off and left me."

"They wouldn't do that. They loved you."

The boxing gloves came closer and began to spar in front of David's nose.

"They were angry. I'd taken the boat out without telling them and my sister was on board."

"I see." David was now beginning to understand something of Jack's agony.

"I got her back in, but the *Neptune* drifted away. Without me."

"But why didn't she drift away immediately?" asked David in bewilderment.

"She was on the lee side of a moored barge, and when I put Sally back on board, the *Neptune* just slipped way."

"Couldn't you have hung on?"

"There wasn't anywhere to grip. Besides, I was so tired."

We're talking, thought David. Properly talking, at last. But he knew he would have to hurry or his mother would come up. "I've been speaking to Matthew. Matthew Trent."

"What for?" Jack's voice was threatening and the gloves came nearer.

"He reckons he saw Sally. She was working in a Chinese take-away."

"At her age?" One of the gloves gave David a nasty clip on the ear.

"She's older. Time has passed, Jack. You're dead. Get it?"

"Stop lying to me."

"Why do you think you've been here all this time? Why do you think no one ever came for you?" David knew he had to reach Jack somehow, but it was so difficult.

"You're lying. Sally's only a kid. And you took my boat." The glove gave him a whack on the ear that really hurt this time and David lost his temper, lashing out and finding only space. How do you fight a poltergeist, he wondered.

CHAPTER NINE

The other glove hit David on the jaw. "I'll get you!" he yelled, launching himself at his unseen opponent with whirling fists and then tripping and falling flat on the floor again.

Just as he landed, the door opened and Auntie Joan stood on the threshold. The gloves dropped to the floor beside him while Jack's mocking laughter echoed round the room.

"Having a game, dear?"

"What?"

"I heard you talking and laughing." Then she began to stir it. "But I thought your father said this room was out of bounds."

David slowly picked himself up, still furious with Jack. Why should either of them help him? He was so stupid. And yet he knew Jack had saved Jenny.

"Find them then," said the commanding voice. "You're not doing enough. I want my mum and dad, and I want Sally."

"OK," said David. 'I'll get back to you."

"Make it fast."

"What's that, dear?"

David had quite forgotten about Auntie Joan. "Er, I said I'll get back downstairs. I only came in because I thought there was a noise and then I tripped over these gloves."

"I don't know why your father doesn't clear this up and give everything to Oxfam. He'll never find those Frasers, you know." She turned her broad backside to him and began to walk out of the door. Then David saw one of the boxing gloves lifting high in the air.

"No, Jack," he whispered. "Don't do it!"

"The old bag." He could hear the poltergeist's withering tones quite clearly.

"Wait!"

Travelling at considerable speed, the boxing glove hit Auntie Joan squarely on the bum, drew back again and then belted her even harder than before. Then it dropped soundlessly to the floor.

"Well, really!"

"It wasn't me."

"I beg your pardon!" She was furious, holding her backside, red in the face and regarding David with accusing eyes. "How could you?"

"It wasn't me." He stuck to the impossible denial.

"Who else could it be?"

"I– I–"

"How dare you!" Her voice was raised in fury. "How dare you assault an old woman! The trouble is that this family shows no respect. No respect at all. I shall leave first thing in the morning."

"But Auntie Joan—" David was desperate.

She went out, opened her bedroom door and slammed it loudly, leaving him standing hopelessly outside.

He went back into Jack's room. "Right," he said. "That's it. I'm not helping you any longer."

Then he saw him, small and vulnerable, crouched under the windowsill.

"You've got to," said Jack.

"No way."

"I'm sorry," he wailed, his pale eyes on David's.

"You've blown it this time. You've really blown it."

"I helped you."

"Now you've got me into trouble. Big trouble."

Finding his apology was too late, Jack took refuge in his normal aggression. "I don't care. I don't care what I do. Unless you find my family, it'll get worse. I can be worse than this. Much worse." Jack began to cry, rubbing his fists into his eyes, and David's heart softened.

"We'll try," he said. "I promise you we'll try. But you've got to stop all this."

He closed the door on Jack's tears and began to run down the two flights of stairs. His mother was standing at the bottom.

"What was all that noise?" she asked wearily. "And was that Auntie Joan's door I heard banging shut? Again."

"You're not going to like this," said David.

"Try me."

"I know I shouldn't have gone into – into that little room, but I saw a pair of boxing gloves in there and I fancied messing around with them."

"Yes." She wasn't sympathetic.

"I was sparring against the door."

"Yes?"

"It opened and Auntie Joan came in."

"You mean—" His mother looked at him in horror, no doubt imagining her sister-in-law with a huge black eye.

"Luckily she turned round quickly."

"And?"

"I got her in the bum."

"David!" His mother stared at him and then her lips quivered. She began to laugh – and went on laughing almost hysterically until she got back to the living room and slumped on to the sofa.

"She'll never forgive us," Mrs Golding said, the laughter dying away at last but her eyes still full of tears. "How could you be so stupid?"

"I'm sorry, Mum."

"I'll go up and–"

"I wouldn't." David was afraid for her. Jack might do something. "Let her sleep on it."

"On a bruised backside?" She began to laugh again.

David tossed and turned, quite unable to sleep, remembering the river and how Jenny could have drowned if it hadn't been for Jack. He had proved he did have a good side to him – but also such a bad one. If he and Jenny were to restore peace in the house, there was no doubt that they would have to trace the Frasers fast. If Jenny was up to it tomorrow, they could check out the Chinese take-away and see if they could follow up any leads.

Gradually, restlessly, David slept and began to dream. At first the dream was familiar. The *Neptune* was sailing up the Thames, but her paint-work was different and her sails spanking new in the light summer breeze. The sky was a cloudless blue and the tide was in, right up to the wharves.

He was standing on one of them, watching the *Neptune* on a run, her main sail out at right angles and the wake streaming from her stern. Behind the tiller was Jack, sturdy in shorts and a T-shirt. A big man with a beard whom David took to be Mr

Fraser was holding the foresail sheet and a beautiful woman with sandy hair was holding a young blonde girl close to her.

"You can forget all your troubles out here," David heard Mr Fraser saying to his wife.

But she only shook her head. "I just take them with me," she replied, staring out at a dredger. "What are we going to do? We could be bankrupt in a few months."

"Don't worry, Mum," said Jack. "Something will come up. I promise."

His father nodded. "We're optimists," he said, "Jack and I."

"Yes," she replied. "That's the trouble."

The craft sped on towards a bend in the river and vanished, but for David, the dream continued. Suddenly he was lost in a maze of back streets, hemmed in with faceless people. Then he found himself swimming, the streets now big ships with blind portholes. Jenny was ahead of him, lying on her back in a life jacket, but when he got nearer he saw that it wasn't Jenny after all but a little blonde girl who was beginning to struggle and call for help.

"Come on, Dave," said Jack. "I'll race you."

David tried his best, but it was no good. He soon found himself sinking below the water, which seemed thin and insubstantial. Down and down he went until he was lying on the sandy bottom, surrounded by Jack's toys. A tall woman slid towards him across the sand, bubbles coming from her mouth. Then he saw that she was Auntie Joan, wearing boxing gloves. She hit David harder and harder round the face, and as the pain grew worse Auntie Joan laughed like his mother and then bubbled at him, "Don't worry. Something will come up."

"David!" There was a voice on the surface of the river. "David." He looked up and saw his mother. "David."

But he couldn't move because he was trapped in the sand, which was slowly rising over his head and suffocating him.

Then he felt his mother pulling off the duvet under which he was buried. "You've had an awful dream," she said. "You've been banging your head on the wall and then disappearing under the duvet. It's all been too much."

But all David could ask in a blurred, sleep-surfacing voice was, "What's that smell?"

"I don't know," she admitted. "It's all over the house."

It was terrible, like rotten eggs.

"It reminds me of something," said his mother. "Something to do with being a child. I know – stink bombs."

"Don't look at me, Mum," said David indignantly. "I was asleep, having a bad nightmare. Remember?"

She nodded. "I bet you it's something to do with that boy's room again. If only your father could at least have gone through all that stuff. I'm sure he would have found some old stink bombs. I expect they went off in the heat."

She sounds like Dad, David thought – looking for a rational explanation at all costs. But then he asked himself, what else could either of them do if they didn't know the truth as he and Jenny did?

"Get dressed," she said. "Unless you don't feel–"

"I'm fine." In fact, he had a splitting headache and wanted Jenny to be back. It was as if half of him had been gone for some time. Besides, if Jack was stepping up his attack – and the stink bomb episode seemed to indicate that he was – David desperately needed her to help him cope with this unpredictable poltergeist. If they didn't find Jack's family soon, he was quite sure that something really dreadful was going to happen.

"I'll go and see if Auntie Joan's up yet," his mother said. "She'll probably see this frightful smell as another insult."

She did. When David was dressed and had come out on the landing, he saw that Auntie Joan was standing at the top of the stairs in a heavy coat and flanked by two suitcases. His mother was pleading with her from the bottom.

"Joan. It can all be explained. David made a terrible mistake and didn't mean to–"

"You're all as bad as each other," she said. "I'm going back to Teddington. At least an old woman can feel safe there. When Reg comes in, you can tell him I've gone."

"At least have some breakfast."

"Here?" she exclaimed. "Have breakfast here?"

Too late, David saw that the toilet door had opened and the tissue was snaking from its holder and wrapping itself around Auntie Joan's feet.

"Watch out," said David.

"Joan!" bellowed his mother. "Have you been to the toilet?"

"How dare you ask me such a personal question!" she fumed. "Are you out of your mind?"

"It's just that you must have caught your heel in the toilet roll," Mrs Golding said timidly.

"What are you talking about?" snapped Auntie Joan.

"You've got toilet paper wrapped round your ankles," said David.

Auntie Joan looked down at her feet. Then she screamed in rage. "How dare you!"

"I'm afraid you must have caught your heel–"

Mrs Golding repeated as Auntie Joan began to pitch forward, almost in slow motion. David grabbed her from behind and together they toppled to the landing floor.

CHAPTER TEN

David was sure he heard Jack's laughter. Inwardly cursing him, he tried to extricate himself from Auntie Joan, but the still unwinding toilet paper was around both of them now, and the more they kicked, the more they became entangled. This would make a good advert, thought David wildly. We're certainly proving this brand is strong.

"Stop kicking me," she shrilled.

"You're kicking me," David replied indignantly.

They continued to become entangled while Mrs Golding shouted instructions from below. David was sure he could catch more of Jack's irritating laughter and then he heard the turning of a key. The front door flew open and his father and Jenny stood on the threshold, looking happy and re-lieved.

"Blimey," said Mr Golding. "What's this? All-in wrestling with a toilet-paper handicap?"

"David," said his sister reprovingly. "What on earth are you doing to Auntie Joan?"

A taxi was called and Auntie Joan, extricated but with a bit of pink toilet paper still in her hair, walked silently down the path to the gate, the driver carrying her bags and eyeing the toilet paper curiously.

Mrs Golding had told her it was there, but a white-faced Auntie Joan wasn't talking to any of them and she departed in total silence.

"She'll never speak to us again," said Mrs Golding. "Never."

"She'll come round," Mr Golding predicted.

"How?"

"Time heals."

"A hundred years would have to pass after what she's been through," said Mrs Golding.

"We're going for a bike ride," said Jenny as soon as David had told her about the amazing events that had occurred in her absence.

"Are you sure—" their father began.

"Yes, I'm sure. I need some fresh air." It was fortunate that their mother was on the telephone for she would never have agreed.

Once the twins were outside, they looked up at Jack's window.

"Shall we tell him where we're going?" she asked.

"He knows what's happening. Ghosts do," replied David.

"He's not your usual ghost, is he?" said Jenny.

"He's more of a poltergeist. Does that make any difference?"

"I don't think so. He's just a type, that's all."

"Not the nicest type," observed Jenny.

The cricket ball sailed out of Jack's window and landed well clear of her on the grass.

"That's a warning," she said.

"How did he get that back?" David picked up the ball to find it was only slightly warm. Jack must be in a more forgiving mood today – or a more hopeful one. "He must have picked my pocket." Jack's window slowly closed. "He doesn't have to stay in there, does he?"

"He can obviously manage other places," said Jenny. "But only for a short while, maybe. Then he's trapped back in that room again. I haven't thanked him," she remembered suddenly. "How awful! He saved my life and I didn't even say thanks."

"I wouldn't worry. He's caused a lot of trouble as well."

"That's nothing compared with saving a life." She went over and stood under the window. "Jack!"

There was no movement.

"Jack?"

Still no response.

"Please, Jack."

The window opened again but there was no sign of Jack.

"I think he can only be seen when he's at his unhappiest. Seen by us, I mean," said David quietly.

"Jack," said Jenny. "I'm very grateful to you for helping Dave save my life. I'll always remember you for that."

The twins were sure they could feel Jack listening.

"We're going to try and find your sister. Now!"

Still there was no reply. Then a ball came hurtling out of the window and they both ducked. This time it was only a tennis ball. Scrawled on it with a crayon was GET A MOVE ON — OR ELSE!

The Three Kingdoms was down a back street in a run-down part of Hockley. By the time the twins had cycled there, it was just after twelve. The takeaway was open for business, but fortunately there were no customers yet.

"Let me do the talking," said Jenny.

Grudgingly David agreed, for he knew she was better at extracting information.

The boy behind the counter was Chinese, and she thought he looked too young to be helpful. She hoped that there were some older people in the kitchen.

Having ordered two portions of sweet and sour chicken, chow mein and boiled rice, Jenny felt she had bought enough goodwill to ask the favour. "I'm looking for a friend – a friend of my mum's."

"Yes?" The boy gazed at her blankly.

"Blonde. In her early twenties. She used to work here–"

"I can't help you."

"Is there anyone else who could?"

"My father maybe?"

"Could you ask him?"

"I'll get him."

While he was gone, both Jenny and David wondered if they had been too optimistic. After all, they didn't know exactly when Matt had thought he had seen Sally, and there could have been a change of ownership at the take-away since then.

An elderly man came out in a white cotton shirt and dark trousers. He looked composed, efficient and withdrawn. "Can I help you?" he asked gently. "My name is Chang."

"I hope so." Jenny felt her confidence draining away. "My mother has lost contact with the daughter of a friend, and she thinks she might have worked here. Her name was Sally Fraser and she had blonde hair. She–"

"Sally?" He spoke the name with great affection.

We've scored, thought David, the relief flooding through him.

"Yes, Sally. Sally Fraser," replied Jenny eagerly.

"She was a lovely person." His face was wreathed in smiles. "Sally worked with me for many years. Started as a holiday job before she left school. I miss her."

"Do you know where she is, Mr Chang?"

"She left to get married. We all went to the wedding."

"But do you know where she is now?" Jenny could hardly contain her impatience and she could see David was feeling exactly the same.

"Sally emigrated. She went to Australia. With her new husband and her parents."

The shock was total. David was the first to recover. "Do you have their address?"

Mr Chang shook his head. "My wife and I were regretting this only the other day. We are not good correspondents and they changed address many times. Her father went bankrupt."

"Again?" Jenny was shocked.

He smiled sadly. "Mr Fraser took too many risks. He loved to sail boats, not to do business. But I could give you the last address we had."

"It's very good of you," said Jenny mechanically. "Was there a telephone number?"

Mr Chang shook his head. "I'm so sorry I can't help you. We were very fond of Sally. She had a tragic childhood."

"Tragic?"

"Her older brother drowned rescuing her in a boating accident. Sally used to say that his soul was never at peace."

"Did she?" David tried not to sound too eager in case he put the man off. "How did she make that out?"

"She was a . . . a sensitive person. She could feel his unrest, perhaps. She worried that he might never have known he did manage to rescue her – that although the boat drifted away, she was safe inside it. She was so young at the time. In fact, I remember Sally once said to me, 'I'm sure Jack never knew whether I survived or not.' "

Jenny was trembling with excitement and frustration. "They wouldn't have come home from Australia? Perhaps if Mr Fraser went bankrupt again–"

Mr Chang shrugged. "If Sally had come back, I'm sure she would have contacted us. We were close friends."

There seemed nothing else to do. Jenny thanked

him, and silently and sadly they went out to their bikes.

"So that's it," David said.

"We've got to explain all this to him," said Jenny. "He'll understand. He'll be reasonable."

"Can poltergeists emigrate?" David asked with sudden enthusiasm.

"Maybe spiritually," she replied doubtfully. "But I think he's trapped."

"Do you reckon Jack can't rest because he thinks his family have left him, or because he doesn't know whether he rescued his sister or not?" David brightened. "If it's that, we can tell him that she did survive – she married and went to Australia."

"You'd think a spirit would know that," said Jenny gloomily.

"Not this one. He's guilty, isn't he? Jack knows he should never have taken a young child out on his own, so maybe he's suffering for it."

"Then it would help if he knew she's alive." Jenny was much more optimistic now.

"He'd want it proved," said David. "You know what Jack's like."

She did. But how could they prove Sally's survival? Would Jack listen to Mr Chang? Or would Mr Chang talk to a poltergeist? Would they get on? She exploded with exhausted laughter and

David crossly asked her what the joke was. When she told him, he was not amused.

David and Jenny cycled home, perplexed and anxious, wondering what they would find on their return. One thing was clear, sooner or later Jack was going to be furious.

Their mother was in the kitchen preparing lunch when the twins arrived.

"Did you hear from Auntie Joan?" asked David curiously.

"She phoned to say she's never been so insulted in her life and she's never going to speak to us again."

"Oh, dear," said Jenny.

"Then she phoned again."

"I thought she said she'd never–" David began.

"She said that she thought David was a very brave boy to rescue his sister and she wanted to know how Jenny was. Because of his bravery she was going to forgive him and forgive us all. She said she'd come back next week to finish off her holiday, but if any more tricks were played on her, she would–"

"Never speak to us again," the twins finished in chorus.

They exchanged glances; they would have to solve Jack's problem before Auntie Joan returned, for there was no doubt that if they didn't, more tricks would be played – and the tricks might get even nastier.

CHAPTER ELEVEN

After lunch Mr Golding and Matthew Trent went back to their usual weekend overtime in the garden centre and Mrs Golding decided to clean out one of the greenhouses. David and Jenny offered to work too, partly because they wanted to help and partly to put off confronting Jack in his room. The centre was due to open in a fortnight and there was still a tremendous amount to do, but their father wouldn't have it. "Take a break – you both deserve it," he said, smiling, and their mother predictably warned them not to "go near that awful boat."

Instead, they hesitantly went up to the awful room.

Fearfully, David opened the door and then drew back.

"It's freezing cold," he said.

He went in slowly and Jenny followed, amazed at the chill that seemed to hang in the air. The space was still and the toys lay scattered around as usual. The twins waited apprehensively for something to happen, but nothing did. Not a toy moved, nor was there any indication at all of Jack's presence.

"You don't think he's gone, do you?" asked Jenny at last.

"Why should he? Nothing's been resolved."

"Maybe he was released. Maybe he knows about Sally now."

David shivered. "I'm sure he doesn't. I think the cold means he's getting more desperate."

Jenny sniffed the air. "What's that smell?"

"Not another stink bomb!"

"No." She was impatient. "It's . . . it's something else."

David sniffed too. "I know what it is – it's the smell of the river. Weed and salt and oil."

"What does it mean?"

"It means he's out searching for her," said David intuitively.

"He must be getting desperate," Jenny replied. "And the more desperate he gets, the more dangerous he's going to be."

Taking care to avoid their parents and Matt, David and Jenny went down to the wharf and immediately made a discovery. The *Neptune* had disappeared.

"So he's taken her out. That must be a first," said David.

"I'm surprised he needs a boat. I thought spirits wandered freely."

"Don't forget he got Sally back into the *Neptune*," Jenny reminded him. "The boat's all part of Jack's mystery."

"Let's go along the bank. Maybe we'll spot him. A boat sailing on its own should attract quite a crowd."

A dusty, overgrown path wound along the sides of wharves, deserted warehouses, a couple of rotting jetties, and wasteland where foliage had grown up among the derelict cars, old tyres and the wreckage of a couple of small cranes. A rabbit scampered into the bushes and an early bumblebee buzzed over some daffodils which had pushed their way through the debris. Nature was claiming the dockland back.

"There she is," said Jenny as they rounded a corner.

The tide was out and the *Neptune* was lying on the mud, her sail still and her boom at right angles. There was hardly any wind but the water was gradually creeping towards her hull.

"If we don't board her now," said David, "we might lose her completely. She could drift out to sea."

"Or more likely be smashed up."

"We'll have to get her back," said David.

"There's not much wind but—" He glanced at his sister and hesitated. "Do you think you can go on board? Sail in the *Neptune* again?"

"Of course I can," replied Jenny emphatically.

"You sure? I mean, I can sail her back if you like."

"Why should I like that?" she rapped. "I've got to get back on board some time, haven't I? What's wrong with now?"

"Jack might be there."

"Yes."

"I mean, it could be a trap," said David. "He may be lying in wait for us."

They studied the *Neptune* warily. A gull flew down and lighted on her mast. Almost immediately it took off again, soaring upwards with what seemed to the twins a startled cry.

"See what I mean?" said David.

"That gull could have been startled by anything," replied Jenny, but she glanced round apprehensively. River traffic was light and no one was on the shore.

"Let's get on with it," said David at last. He clambered over an old wooden flood barrier and Jenny followed, but once on the mud they paused again.

"Can't see anything," said David.

"He is a ghost," muttered Jenny.

"Poltergeists are usually pretty active," her brother replied defensively. "As we've seen."

But nothing moved, and the boat was utterly still as the incoming tide lapped up to her hull.

The mud was soft and clinging, but Jenny and David soon made it to the *Neptune*.

"I'll go on board first," he said with some qualms.

"No way." Jenny clambered up and sat on the starboard side.

Hesitantly, David joined her. "Jack," he whispered and then more loudly, "Jack?"

There was no reply, but when Jenny touched the deck she cried out in pain. "Feel this – it's freezing cold."

"I'm sure all this cold means he's getting desperate. Aren't you, Jack? Can you hear me, Jack?" But there was still no reply.

The tide was now creeping under the bow of the *Neptune* which was gently rocking.

"It'll be dead easy to sail her back," said David.

"Easy?" questioned Jenny. "And I don't like your use of the word 'dead'."

They both strained their ears for the sound of Jack's laughter, but there was only the lapping of the tide.

"I'll take the helm," said Jenny.

"OK."

They were both very tense as the tide lifted them and the sail of the *Neptune* filled with the gentlest of breezes. Jenny steered her out into the stream and set sail for home.

"There's a tug with a couple of barges up ahead," said David.

"OK. I'll come in a bit."

Suddenly the sail billowed out, but there was no wind.

"Look at that," said David in awe.

"Ready about," said Jenny as the *Neptune* veered round.

"You can't do that," yelled her brother. "You'll be heading for the tug."

"I don't have any choice," she replied.

"No choice. No wind. It's Jack," said David.

The *Neptune* was now heading at considerable speed for the tug and its two barges.

"Jack!" yelled Jenny. "Stop it."

"Where are they?" The voice seemed to come from the water. "Where are my parents?"

"In Australia."

"And Sally?"

"She's there too. She's married. We found out this morning but you'd gone."

"You're lying."

"No!"

"Oh yes, you are. Dad and Mum wouldn't have left me. And Sally's dead."

"She's not. We can prove it."

"She's dead!" The voice from the water was insistent.

"We talked to a man in a Chinese take-away. Sally used to work there. He can tell you. Mr Chang can prove it all to you."

"It was my fault – it's all my fault." There was a sob in Jack's voice.

"She's alive," David insisted. Now they were getting near the tug. Too near.

"And you're lying about my parents."

The tug gave a warning blast.

"Your parents are in Australia, Jack," said Jenny as calmly as she could. "Please turn us about, or we'll hit the tug."

The crew was crowding on to the deck, amazed at seeing a small craft in full sail when there was no wind.

"You're lying. They wouldn't have left me."

"You're dead, Jack," yelled David. "How many times do we have to tell you? Can't you get it through your thick head? You drowned rescuing your sister. Don't you remember? You're a hero! A real hero."

They were only metres from the tug now. Its

hooter was blasting at them and the men on the deck were shouting.

"Please, Jack!" screamed Jenny. "Please help us! Like you did last time."

"If I'm drowned, show me my grave," came the voice. "Bring me a photograph. I'll give you one more day. If you don't find my parents and my sister – you'll be dead."

"Like you?" David yelled.

It wasn't the most tactful question and the *Neptune* sailed on.

"Say I'm not dead," Jack insisted.

"You're *not* dead," David conceded quickly.

Still the *Neptune* sailed on.

"Jack!" Jenny shrieked.

At the very last moment, the boat veered away from the bow of the tug and came to a halt, wildly rocking in its wake as the sail went limp.

"That was close." David was trembling un-controllably.

"Too close," agreed Jenny. "Thanks, Jack," she remembered to say.

There was no reply.

David was also anxious to placate him. "Thanks a lot, Jack."

The rocking gently subsided.

Jenny helmed the *Neptune* towards home slowly

and safely. There were no further incidents nor any indication of the poltergeist's presence.

"So we've got a day," said Jenny gloomily. "He's set us an impossible deadline. Typical."

"Twenty-four hours – and a photograph to take."

"We don't even know where he's buried – if at all."

"Matt might."

"But what are we going to do?" Jenny was beginning to panic and she could see that David was in much the same state. "Nothing will ever satisfy him and he'll kill us in the end – I know he will."

"The photograph may calm him down." But he knew he was being optimistic.

"It won't. He's obsessed."

"So what do we do? Go to Australia?"

Jenny laughed mirthlessly. "There's nothing we can do. Except plead with Jack."

"I don't think he's pleadable with," remarked her brother.

As they quickly and quietly moored the *Neptune* on the rising tide, David looked at his watch and saw that it was just after five.

"Do you reckon Jack's grave might be in the

cemetery?" he suggested tentatively. "The one at Denlin Hill?"

Jenny shrugged. 'Maybe. It's the biggest round here."

"If his grave is there, we could photograph it tonight. We'd have all day tomorrow to work out what we're going to do."

"Before Jack kills us?" said Jenny.

"He won't do anything of the kind." David was stoic. "We're the only people who can help him – and he knows it." Then he shivered. "But I guess he'll make life pretty tough."

"Yes," said Jenny grimly. "He's vicious enough in the house but once he gets outside it seems to go to his head. Must be the fresh air."

David nodded. "I know what you mean," he said with feeling. "Look – there's Matt on his own. Let's get to him before Dad or Mum turn up."

"You're muddy," said Matthew Trent, leaning on his spade with the sweat standing out on his brow. "What you been up to?"

"The *Neptune* slipped her moorings," said David. "We just brought her back."

"Well done. You be careful, though."

"Yes."

"After what happened."

"It's rather like falling off a horse," Jenny replied abruptly. "You've got to get back on again fast."

"We're still wondering about Jack," said David slowly.

"Yes?"

"Do you know if he was buried somewhere round here?"

"Getting morbid, aren't you?"

"Well–"

"And obsessed with the poor lad."

"Just interested," said David. "Interested and . . . we got kind of fond of him through the *Neptune*."

"His photograph's on his gravestone," said Matt unexpectedly. "Don't approve of that myself. Continental idea. Know what I mean?"

"Yes," said Jenny trying to encourage him.

"It's up at Denlin. You thinking of going there?"

"We might. One day."

"The grave's in the third row, on the right as you come in. Right down the end."

"Do you ever go?"

"I sometimes take a look. My old dad's buried nearby."

"Anyone ever kept up Jack's grave?" asked Jenny with sudden inspiration.

There was a long pause. Then Matt said, "Funny you should say that. There were fresh flowers on it last time I went and the whole grave's been tidied up, like."

"How amazing!" said Jenny. "The owner of that take-away said the whole family'd gone to Australia."

Matt shrugged. "You are a couple of Sherlock Holmeses, aren't you? Must be uncles and aunts then," he added, returning to his digging.

"Of course," said David, disappointed, but as he glanced at Jenny he felt a surge of excitement. What idiots they were! Complete idiots. If there were relatives, then they must be able to get in touch with the Frasers in Australia. Why on earth hadn't they thought about that before? Why had they allowed Jack to tyrannise them to such an extent that they could no longer think straight?

CHAPTER TWELVE

"You OK?" asked David.

"I'm knackered," Jenny replied. "I didn't get much sleep in that hospital last night."

"I bet you didn't. Maybe we should turn back."

It was a long ride to the cemetery through the traffic-filled streets and he could see that she was tired.

"No way," she replied determinedly. "I'm not going back, whatever happens. Besides, it's not far now."

But it was and they had to puff up a long hill before they reached the cemetery gates, which stood out startlingly in the spring twilight. They were wrought iron and gilded, with the name HOCKLEY CEMETERY picked out in gold leaf on the top. Behind them were rows and rows of graves, tombs, mausoleums and family vaults – an imposing, eerie sight in the still of the evening.

They followed Matt's directions and eventually found the grave. The tombstone was simple and striking. Jack looked very familiar in the photograph, and stared out at them with his cherubic smile and tousled hair. The inscription read:

TO OUR BELOVED SON
JACK (JOHN) DEREK FRASER
DIED GALLANTLY AT TWELVE.
MAY HE REST IN PEACE WITH
LOVE IN HIS HEART. 1969—1981

Jenny's eyes filled with tears and David felt a strong pricking at the back of his own lids.

"Pity it doesn't read, 'Died gallantly at twelve saving his sister Sally'," said David shakily.

"Yeah." Jenny sniffed. Then she got out her camera and took several shots. "It's a good likeness, that photo."

"Yes. Yes, it is."

"And the grave is well kept up."

It was neatly trimmed and planted with pansies of almost every colour. There was also a bunch of daffodils just under the headstone.

"There's a label," said David. "That could give us a clue."

They turned it over carefully and gazed at the neat writing in complete amazement. It read, "To dear Jack, with love and gratitude always. Sally."

David reeled back. "Sally," he whispered. "It can't be possible."

"She came back?"

"Wait a minute." David felt a pang of frustration. "She could have sent these from Australia via Interflora, or she could have asked someone to buy the flowers and write the label."

Jenny stared at him, looking betrayed. "Oh, no!"

"It's possible."

"Not after all this effort." She looked at the handwriting again but could tell nothing from it.

Then David saw the grave digger – an old man slowly and not very effectively excavating a fresh grave. "Would he know?"

"Know what?"

"Whether Sally comes here," said David impatiently.

"Why should he?" Jenny asked miserably. She was feeling completely defeated.

"It's worth a try."

David hurried over to the grave digger and Jenny followed.

"Excuse me."

The old man continued his digging.

"Excuse me."

"Well?" He didn't even bother to look up.

"Er, Jack Fraser's grave."

There was no reply.

"Do you know the one?" asked Jenny.

Still no reply.

"Do you know–"

He interrupted her testily. "There's hundreds of graves here. Can't be expected to know each one, can I?"

"Of course not. I just wondered."

For the first time he looked up, his face red and sweaty. "Relation?"

"A friend," said David.

"He's a bit before your time." The grave digger looked at him warily.

"Friend of the family, we mean." David tried to pull himself together.

"What do you want to know?"

"A lady comes. In her twenties. Sally Fraser, I mean."

"I know the one," said the old man and a thrill passed through the twins. But they both knew they shouldn't raise their hopes yet. "What do you want with her?"

"We haven't seen her for years and we noticed she'd put those lovely flowers on Jack's grave – and we wanted to meet up with her again."

"Used to come."

"Used to?" wailed David.

"Regular as clockwork. Then she stopped."

"And that's it?" Jenny was distraught.

"Then she started coming again."

"Wow!" said David.

Jenny could hardly trust herself to believe what the old man had just said. "When was this?" she asked eagerly.

"Four weeks ago. Maybe a bit more," he corrected himself. "Comes regular as clockwork Sundays. Hasn't been today yet, though."

"What time does she come?" David thought he was going to pass out, the relief was so great.

"Tea-time usually. If you hang around a bit you might just catch her."

"And you're sure she's Sally Fraser?"

"Of course I'm sure." He looked indignant. "I don't get my facts wrong like you youngsters nowadays. We was brought up to be reliable."

"But please, please tell us how you can be sure." Jenny looked so vulnerable that the crotchety old grave digger gave her a tired smile.

"I asked her. I don't normally presume, but in this case – I thought I recognised her. Anyway, she's a charming lady. Didn't mind at all. Said she'd been in Australia with her parents and husband but it didn't work out so well. Her parents stayed, but she and her husband came home. They run a newsagent's shop somewhere in the town."

Jenny could have hugged him. "Thank you so much," she said enthusiastically.

"You certainly found out a lot in a short time, didn't you?" said David rather tactlessly.

"I hope you're not implying I'm prone to gossip," said the old man, glaring at him.

"Oh, no!" David quickly backed down. "It's just that we're so grateful – that's all."

"It's good to see a grave so well cared for," said the old man. "Too many get neglected."

"We've done it!" said Jenny after they had thanked the grave digger yet again. "We've actually done it."

"Jack should be pleased," David said. "Or is he going to insist on the whole family?"

"Somehow I think he's going to be satisfied with Sally. Particularly Sally alive."

The waiting seemed interminable, but eventually the twins saw a woman coming up the path, carrying a basket. As she came nearer, Jenny and David could see she was quite short with blonde hair.

"She must be Sally," said David feverishly. "Do you want to do the talking?"

"I'll try."

They waited until the woman reached the grave. She put her basket down, took out a trowel and began to trim up the edges, her lips moving slightly at the same time. Was she talking to Jack, David wondered.

"Excuse me," said Jenny, suddenly realising her explanation was going to sound so weird that she didn't know where to start.

"Yes?" The woman got to her feet with a smile. "How can I help you?" Immediately they could both see that she had a strong likeness to Jack. Maybe it was going to be all right after all.

"Are you Sally – Sally Fraser?"

"I was."

"Jack's sister?"

"That's right. Who are you?" She was still smiling and she didn't seem in the least suspicious or put out. Jenny began to feel more confident.

"We're Jenny and David Golding – and we live at River House."

"River House?" Sally Fraser's face clouded.

"Was it your parents who left Jack's room just as it was?" continued Jenny.

"They couldn't bear to–"

"My parents have left it just as it was, too."

Sally stared at them, her lips working but no sound coming out. Then she said, "Thank you. That was good of you. I'll come and collect the stuff, if I may. Unless you want to give it to charity. Technically, of course, you've bought it all so I suppose–"

"We'd like you to collect it," said Jenny. "I know my parents would. But you'd come yourself, wouldn't you? You wouldn't mind going into his room again?"

Sally looked thoughtful. "No. Obviously it would be painful. Very painful. But I don't mind. How did you know about me?"

Jenny nodded to the grave digger, who was pretending to dig but was in fact peering intently at them.

"Old Ned. Of course."

"You see, we've seen him."

"Ned?" She looked puzzled.

"Jack."

"What?" Sally looked even more puzzled.

"Yes. He's been naughty – well, I mean, I suppose poltergeists often are."

"Poltergeist?"

"Jenny–" David tried to intervene, to stop the calamity hurtling towards them with the same ferocity as Jack's cricket ball.

"Let me go on, please. He threw all his toys at us – well, some of them, and did terrible things to our Auntie Joan. Then he knocked me over the side of the boat."

"You mean the *Neptune*?" breathed Sally.

"That's right. But he did help David to save me. Then the next day he almost made us run into a

tug. He thinks you drowned, Sally. It's an obses-
sion with him. And he wants to know why his
parents deserted him."

"But—"

"Yes, I know. He's dead. But Jack doesn't think
he's dead. Honestly, he doesn't. And he's given us
just a day to find you – and his parents."

To his horror David could see Sally Fraser's
expression hardening.

"This is all a bit much to take in, isn't it?" he
said desperately. "Why don't you come home
with us?"

"Come home with you?" Even Jenny could see
that Sally Fraser was angry. "I wouldn't dream of
doing that."

"But why not?" Jenny was floundering.

Sally was flushed and shaking with emotion.
"How could you play a joke like this on me? And
whilst I was tending his grave."

"It's not a joke," said David.

"Of course it isn't." Jenny was horrified. "Please
believe us."

"Do you really live at River House, or did you
make all this up?"

"We can prove it," said David desperately.

"If you do, I suppose you managed to find out
about poor Jack. And now you're making a joke
of it." Her voice shook.

"These kids bothering you, madam?" The grave digger was standing beside them now.

"Yes. Yes, they are."

Jenny was frantic. "We're just trying to explain," she said. "That's all."

"It's all true," David tried to assure her. "Every word is true."

"You horrible little liars!"

"No!"

"How dare you bother me! How dare you make up this tasteless joke!" Sally Fraser was white with rage now.

"We're not liars!" yelled David.

"And don't shout!"

"We're not," he said more quietly.

Sally gathered up her basket and put the trowel inside, shivering with a mixture of anger and shock. "Don't ever speak to me again."

"You've got to come to the house – to his room," said David, trying to be calmer.

"I wouldn't dream of it."

"You have to collect Jack's things."

"Send them to a charity." She was beginning to walk away down the path now.

"Wait!" sobbed Jenny.

"No," replied Sally. "You wait. I'm sure Mr Morrison will stop you following me."

"I certainly will, madam."

"These children have played a cruel joke on me." Sally was in tears now.

"It's all a misunderstanding," said David.

"You must listen to us," pleaded Jenny.

"I never want to see you again," shouted Sally over her shoulder. "Do you understand?"

"I understand," said Mr Morrison aggressively. "You're staying here until the lady's out of sight. I ought to call the police and have you arrested. As it is, if I ever see you in this cemetery again, I will call them. Now stay here!"

They waited until Sally was out of sight.

On the way back to River House, David was determined not to blame Jenny for her impulsiveness. But he didn't have to.

"If only I hadn't been stupid enough to go on trying to explain," said Jenny miserably. "If she'd just come to his room I'm sure it would have been enough – more than enough. It was when I tried to convince her that Jack was a poltergeist that she went bananas."

"We could find out where she lives. Talk to her again," suggested David.

"Who from? That old grave digger will call the police if he sees us again."

"Maybe she'll go to Mr Chang."

"And what good would that do?"

"He'd know her address."

"Yes – and you can imagine what she'd say to Mr Chang about us. He'd never speak to us again, either. We could probably trace her eventually by checking out all the newsagents. But even if we do find her she won't want to talk now. It's all my fault!"

"Maybe Jack will understand," said David dolefully.

"That selfish little brute? He just wants what he wants, and he doesn't care how he gets it. He'll terrorise the house now and we'll all have to leave. Dad will lose his job and so will Matt, and Jack will have lost another family and we'll all end up living somewhere horrible – while that little twit haunts River House for ever. And I even feel sorry for him."

"I don't," said David fiercely.

"Anyway, it's all my fault." Jenny was wobbling on her bike as they took the turning home. "You wait and see what Jack will do now."

CHAPTER THIRTEEN

After supper, having been soundly admonished by their mother for being late back, David and Jenny cautiously climbed the stairs to Jack's room, conscious that both their parents were watching TV but might come upstairs at any minute.

"Keep quiet," whispered Jenny. "You're making too much noise."

"Let me speak to him," hissed David.

"No! I made the mistake so I'll take the consequences." She tried to open the door and muffled a cry of anguish.

"What now?"

"The knob's freezing."

David tried; he gritted his teeth, giving a little moan of pain, and failed completely to open the door.

"He must be angry," said Jenny.

"Too bad. We've got to stand up to him. We can't let Jack rule us like this." David was becoming furious with himself. "If he thinks he can bully us, then he'll get even worse."

Jenny suddenly smiled at her brother. "You're right, Dave. Absolutely right. I've been panicking."

She tried the doorknob again to find that it was much warmer. Briskly she opened it.

Jack was sitting under the windowsill, a football in his hands. His eyes were menacing, but both David and Jenny could also see the fear and panic in them.

The room was deadly cold, despite the fact that the window was closed.

"We've got good news for you," said David.

"What is it?" he asked ungraciously.

"We've seen Sally," said Jenny. "Met and talked with her." She decided against saying where, since Jack always denied being dead.

"Where?"

"The man in the Chinese–" Jenny stopped herself, knowing she couldn't lie to him.

"We went to your grave," said David bluntly. "That's where we met her." The football slammed towards him but he ducked in time. "You little coward," he said as the football returned to Jack's hands.

But this time there was no smile of triumph on Jack's face, only a look of hatred and desperation.

"It's true," said Jenny. "We went to your grave

and it's got beautiful flowers. The inscription says you died gallantly – bravely – and there's Sally to prove it."

"She talks to you, Jack. She honestly does – and she comes every Sunday. Don't you feel her? Can't you hear? Or have you shut her out? Your parents went to Australia and Sally and her husband went out with them. Your dad and mum are still there but the others came back. They've got a newsagent's in the town. Honestly, Jack, she does talk to you."

"Sometimes I can hear her," he said unexpectedly. "At least I think I can. I thought it was dreams. It probably is."

"You've got to admit something to yourself," said David. "Something difficult. Impossible."

"What's that?" There was a new edge to Jack's voice.

"That you're dead. That you drowned. That people were sorry because they loved you very much. Sally comes to your grave every Sunday. That proves something, doesn't it?"

"I want to see her," said Jack. "Maybe if I see her I'll know."

"That you're dead?"

"How can I be dead if I'm trapped here?" he said. "Sometimes if I'm really angry I can be in my boat – the one you stole – or even other places.

But that's all. I mean, I can't even go to the cinema." His voice ended on a sob. "Can I?"

He certainly had a point, thought David, and he knew Jenny felt the same.

"Why am I trapped here?" asked Jack.

"Maybe it's because you won't accept that you drowned," said Jenny.

But Jack sat under the windowsill, clutching the football, and David and Jenny knew for a certainty that his only chance of release lay in seeing Sally with his own ghostly eyes.

"I've got to see her," said Jack, as if voicing their thoughts.

"There's a problem about that," said Jenny slowly and unwillingly.

"What problem?" The poltergeist scowled sulkily and threateningly.

"She won't come here."

"Why not?"

"I made a mistake," said Jenny. "A big mistake."

"It wasn't Jenny's fault," interrupted David defensively. "So don't you go blaming her, Jack." He watched the large leather football that Jack was turning over and over in his ghostly hands. That could hurt.

"What happened?" he asked softly.

"I told her you were a ghost and she wouldn't

believe me. Sally got angry and walked away. She thought we were teasing her in some horrible way, but of course we weren't."

Jack got up and the room became colder and darker. "Of course she walked away." His voice grated in anger. "Wouldn't you, if someone asked you to meet a ghost?"

"I was telling the truth," protested Jenny. "You are a ghost."

Jack vanished, but the football remained in mid-air. The cold intensified and the room grew so dark they could hardly see each other.

"Jack," said Jenny warningly. "You'll never get anywhere this way."

"We need your co-operation." David was more afraid than he had ever been. "If you don't give it to us, you'll never find her."

The silence was absolute.

"All right," said Jenny. "We're not putting up with this. We'll come back when you're less bad-tempered."

The silence seemed to increase until it became a thick wall. Then David turned away from the still hovering football and tried the door handle. It wouldn't move. He tried it again, but it was frozen, becoming colder and colder by the second until he let it go with a cry of pain.

Jenny tried, but it was no good; they were locked in and the icy feel of the doorknob seemed to penetrate right inside them.

"Stop playing games, Jack," she said sharply. "If we can talk this over sensibly, I'm sure we'll be able to persuade Sally to come here."

"Games?" came a hard voice from nowhere. "I like games."

"Shut up, you spoilt little brat," David said angrily. "We're fed up with being bullied by you."

"Will you play a game with me?"

"No chance," said David.

"Well, you can't get out – so you'll have to."

Still the football hovered in mid-air. Then Jenny noticed something: it was smoking. "Is that ice or fire?" she asked.

"You'll soon find out."

The ball flew at her so fast that the twins could only see a blur. Jenny jumped aside but the ball grazed her and she could feel its heat. It spiralled, circled and hurled itself at David, but he trapped and kicked it hard at the wall, wincing with pain as he felt the burning sensation through his trainers. The ball crashed to the floor and the clockwork monkey stood up, banging its drum with a mechanical beat as columns of model soldiers marched towards them.

A boxing glove caught David under the chin as Jenny was pelted with marbles. Then the column of soldiers brought the twins down, while a nylon fishing line curled around their feet and hovering tubes of oil paint squeezed themselves over their heads and clothes.

"Stop it, Jack!" David yelled above the noise of the monkey beating his drum. "I'll fix you for this."

"How?" The voice laughed.

"So you do know you're different," panted Jenny. "You knew all the time."

"I don't want to be different," howled the voice, stricken with anguish now. "Why should I want to be different?"

The boxing gloves whacked them both across the chest and Lego rained on them from a considerable height.

"I want my mum and dad," cried Jack. "I don't understand what's happened to me."

"You drowned," said Jenny. "You drowned saving your sister's life. You're a hero and she's grateful. How many times do we have to tell you?"

"If she's so grateful, why isn't she here?"

"Because she doesn't believe us." David was white with anger. "And why should she? She'll never help us; I'll make sure she doesn't. She'll never come to this room, Jack. You'll be here, all alone, for the rest of eternity."

"Eternity! For ever?" Jack broke off hostilities abruptly; he sounded scared again.

"For ever," David repeated bleakly. "Why don't you stop all this? Try and work out a plan with us—"

"I don't trust you."

"You've got to try," said Jenny.

"I want Sally here now!" Jack was working himself up into a rage. 'NOW!"

"It's impossible!" yelled David. "So shut up!"

The boxing glove hit him again, followed by another shower of Lego. Then there was a thundering knock on the door.

"Just what are you two doing making all that noise? We said you weren't to go in there."

Neither Jenny nor David could think of anything to say in reply.

"David! Jenny! What *are* you doing?" Their mother sounded worried and slightly frightened now. "What on earth is going on?"

"Everything started flying around again. We came in to see what was happening."

"Open the door."

"We can't," said Jenny. "We got locked in."

"There's no key! And no lock! What have you done to the door!"

"Try it for yourself," shouted David. "We can't get out and you can't get in."

He was right. She couldn't.

"What's happening?" Their mother was no longer angry but increasingly afraid.

"You'll need to get Dad to break down the door."

"There's someone on the phone."

"The phone?" At a time like this, thought David.

"A Chinese man. I can't keep him hanging on for ever. I think he said his name was Chang."

"Who?" gasped Jenny.

"Chang."

"What's he want?"

"He said he was phoning on behalf of someone called Sally."

"I don't believe it," said David, his hopes soaring.

"I'm sure that's what he said."

"Can't you hear?" snapped Jenny. "Jack, can't you hear?"

"Who?" their mother asked through the door.

The twins felt the cold and darkness recede as Jack relented.

"Get us out of here before he rings off," said David urgently. "This could be your last chance. Get it?"

The fishing line went limp, their bonds parted and David and Jenny, battered and in considerable pain, staggered to the door. It opened immediately.

CHAPTER FOURTEEN

"What have you been doing?" their mother asked, barring the way.

"It's an emergency!" yelled David.

"Don't stop us now." Jenny was already past her. "He may ring off any second–"

"But you're covered in paint–"

"We'll explain later, Mum," said David.

"Did you do that to each other?" She was amazed. "And if so, why? And what about the door?"

But the twins were already half-way down the stairs.

"Cold in there," muttered their mother, staring into the room. But she saw nothing.

"Mr Chang?"

"You have come to the phone at last." His voice was patient.

"I'm sorry," said Jenny. "Mum couldn't find us. You've got a message from Sally?"

"She asked me to ring you."

"Yes?" Jenny was too apprehensive to say any more.

"About coming to see you."

Suddenly, life was full of light again, and as she whispered the news to David he let out a cry of triumph which drew his father away from the TV and their mother down the stairs.

"Sally thought it over and came and had a talk with me," continued Mr Chang. "I was so glad she came. It was all such a shock, your conversation in the cemetery. She thought you were making fun of her."

"We'd never do that," said Jenny.

"I told her I didn't think you were the type. I told her that things can happen – strange things that we can never rationalise. A presence like this – the little boy's soul has not departed. When I spoke like that, Sally was less alarmed. Would you mind if we both came?"

"Mind? I'd – we'd be delighted," said Jenny, overjoyed, the relief making her head spin. "Can you come now?"

"In about twenty minutes."

"You know the way?"

"Sally does."

"Of course," said Jenny. "How stupid of me."

"What's going on?" asked Mrs Golding fiercely. "We've got a right to know."

David took over quickly before Jenny could burst into an explanation, just in case she went on about ghosts again.

"We met Sally Fraser."

"Who?"

"The girl who used to live here. The one who was saved from drowning by her brother."

"So you know about that, do you?" asked their father grimly. "Is this Matt's doing?"

"No. We found out from a man at a Chinese take-away," David admitted, hoping he wasn't going to make too much of a fuss.

"He's got no right—"

"And we met her and she puts flowers on Jack's grave every day and she's really nice and—"

"And?"

"She wants to come round here and take away his toys."

"Ah." Their mother breathed a sigh of relief and their father visibly relaxed.

"Can she, Mum?" asked Jenny.

"You seem to have asked her already," admonished her father.

"We didn't mean to—" began David.

"But you did – without asking us." But their mother still looked relieved. 'I don't mind, though. I'd like her to take the stuff away and then we'll have to think about getting that wiring renewed."

"Yes," agreed their father. "That should do for the static electricity."

Only Sally can do for that, thought Jenny.

"I'll be glad. I suppose," their mother said reflectively, "one of the Frasers should come."

"Why?' asked Jenny, surprised. Had she guessed? Could Mum have seen him too?

"Poor little boy. That's why we didn't tell you – for fear of getting you both upset. As for that boat–" She looked angrily at her husband. "Why, Jenny almost–" Mrs Golding stopped and then continued hurriedly. "I'll be pleased to meet the young lady."

"Can we go and – and start parcelling up the toys?" asked David. "We could use some of those black dustbin bags."

"I should get the paint off your faces first," said Dad. "You look a right sight."

The room was no longer cold. Instead it was fresh and clean-smelling.

Jenny was wondering why her mother was so pleased that a Fraser was coming to the house and, as usual, David knew what his sister was thinking.

"Do you think Mum's got our gift?" he asked.

"Dad certainly hasn't. That I do know," replied Jenny. "But Mum – maybe she senses Jack's unhappiness and thinks that Sally coming might be some kind of exorcism."

"Which it is – I hope," said David.

She nodded. "But I honestly don't think Mum can *see*. Not in our way."

"Wonder if Jack knows what's going on? He's very quiet at the moment."

"You're to behave yourself," said Jenny to thin air, rather as if admonishing a young child before a party. "No fury."

"And no chucking things about," snapped David, gingerly stroking the bruise on his jaw.

There was no reply. Jack was obviously biding his time.

"Do you think Sally being here will do what it's supposed to do?" David asked. "Do you think she can really free Jack?"

"I hope so," said Jenny whole-heartedly.

"Suppose he insists on seeing his parents too?"

"Maybe Sally can help. She's got to."

"She can help you, Jack," said David belligerently, directing his gaze to the windowsill. "Do you hear that? But you've got to treat her right."

There was still no reply but the football rose fractionally in the air and then was still again.

"What's he saying?" asked Jenny.

"Not a lot," replied her brother. "I think he's hedging his bets."

"So are we," she said.

Mr Chang and Sally Fraser stood outside the front door of River House. He was looking protective and she was hesitant. Luckily, Mr Golding wasn't around and his wife was being especially kind and tactful.

"Do come and have a cup of tea after you've been upstairs," she said. "And if you want to look round the house . . ."

"Thank you," said Sally. She was beginning to look anxious, wondering if she had been right to have second thoughts and to give the twins a chance. "I'll – we'll get the toys. I've brought some sacks. I don't know what my parents were doing, leaving all that stuff here."

"Grief," said Mr Chang, and Mrs Golding nodded approvingly. She obviously liked him.

"As this is all Jenny and David's idea, I'll be in the kitchen. Just give me a call if you want anything."

As she withdrew, Mr Chang said quietly, "Shall we go up?"

The moment had come that the twins – and no doubt Sally Fraser – had dreaded most.

Gently, very gently, David tried the handle of Jack's door. The biting cold had returned even more intensely than before and it wouldn't turn.

"He's nervous," said David, rubbing at his hand.

Sally Fraser stared at him as if he was insane. "Look, is all this—"

"It's not easy," said Jenny.

"Let me try." Mr Chang gripped the doorknob, but fell back wincing with the agony of the deadly cold metal.

"This is ridiculous," David snapped. He hammered on the door. "Jack! Let us in."

"If this is a joke—" muttered Sally.

"No," said Mr Chang firmly. "I can assure you that this is no joke whatsoever."

"Let us in, Jack," said Jenny. "It's Sally." She tentatively tried the handle but it was still searingly cold. "I'm sorry," she said. "You'll have to do it."

"I can't." Sally was no longer sceptical but very afraid.

"It's all right. He's not dangerous or anything." Jenny tried to reassure her.

"Much," muttered David.

"Jack's just lonely and confused," she continued sadly. "He doesn't know what's happened to him. I mean, he doesn't really accept that he's dead at all."

Sally turned away, shaking. "I can't take this."

"You must," said Mr Chang. "You really must."

Sally moved away from the door. "But it's all such a shock, I—"

"You've got to try," said David. "You've really got to."

"It'll hurt me." Sally gazed at the handle in terror. "I can't bear it."

"Just try," pleaded Jenny.

"I can't!"

"Please. Not for us – but for Jack."

Sally Fraser hesitated and then reached out.

"It's warm," she said in amazement. "Quite warm."

"That means he wants you," replied Jenny. "Just open the door and go in."

Sally remained where she was.

"Go on," said David. "He won't bite."

Slowly, she turned the handle and the door opened a crack.

"Is it cold?" asked Jenny.

"No," said Sally. "It feels like a summer's day."

Sally still hesitated in the doorway. "I can't go in."

"Please," said Mr Chang.

"I can't!"

"Then I shall go in – on your behalf," he said boldly.

"No," David and Jenny chorused. "You can't do that."

"Why?"

"He's powerful," said Jenny. "Very powerful."

"You said there was nothing to be afraid of," said Mr Chang. "And I am not afraid." He pushed open the door and, before either of the twins could stop him, walked straight into Jack's room.

There was a cry of rage and a sudden flash. The room went pitch dark and numbingly cold – far more than ever before. Then Mr Chang was ejected backwards, ice on his nose and lips, falling down on the landing. Through the open door they could see Jack in his usual place under the windowsill, wide-eyed with rage and loathing.

"Jack?" whispered Sally. "Jack?"

Slowly the icy cold began to disperse.

"Jack?" Sally still hovered on the threshold, gazing at the small figure crouched under the window. Behind her, Mr Chang rose slowly to his feet.

"Sal?" Jack's voice was bewildered and halting, still suspicious.

"It's me. It's really me, Jack."

"You didn't drown?"

"I got picked up by a launch. But you – poor Jack!" Sally gave a sob. "You drowned. What are you doing in this room?"

"I got left behind."

"Come to me, Jack." She opened her arms to

him and he ran at her like a tornado. But there was no impact. Instead, Jack seemed to disappear somewhere inside her and suddenly the room felt empty.

She turned to the twins. "He's come back to me," she whispered. "Jack's come back to me at last."

After Sally Fraser and Mr Chang, now quite recovered but still a little dazed, had finished having tea with a curious but resolutely unquestioning Mrs Golding, the twins accompanied them down the drive.

"I'm sorry I doubted you both," said Sally. "I just had no idea that these things could happen."

"It was a pretty weird story," admitted David.

"Do you think we'll see Jack again?" asked Jenny unsteadily.

Mr Chang shook his head. "He and Sally are reunited now. I don't think you'll have any more of your restless spirit."

"I'll miss him," said Jenny.

"I won't." David was sure of that.

When the visitors had gone, the twins slowly returned to the house. Then David bent down and began to scrabble in the long grass.

"What's up?"

"We've got a souvenir." He retrieved the cricket ball and passed it to Jenny.

"It's warm," she said in surprise.

"Careful. Could be one of his tricks–"

"No." Jenny held the cricket ball tightly as the warmth began to fade. "I think Jack was saying goodbye," she said.

Other titles in the *Ghosthunters* series:

HAUNTED SCHOOL

David went cold all over as the shock hit him.
Sweat broke out on his forehead and his hands
felt clammy. Jenny was right; he could see
straight through the dog . . .

DEADLY GAMES

The twins' shoulders were trembling violently.
Then the whole disused tunnel came alive with
blinding white light . . . Shadows leapt from
the walls and they could just make out
shapes moving, running.
Then a roaring sound seemed to burst through
the walls of the tunnel, echoing so insistently
in their ears it almost hurt . . .